GW01561000

Andrew Pang

The Arch Scar

The Arch Scar
Copyright © 2024 by Andrew Pang
All rights reserved.

No part of this book may be copied, shared, or transmitted in any format or by any method, whether through photocopying, recording, or electronic or mechanical means, without the express written consent of the author, except for brief excerpts used in reviews or other non-commercial purposes allowed by copyright law.

This is a fictional work. While it references certain historical figures, locations, and events, they have been adapted to suit the narrative. Names, characters, settings, and events that are not historical are either products of the author's imagination or used in a fictional context. Any similarities to actual events or individuals, living or deceased, are purely coincidental.

Some locations in this story are based on real places, but certain elements have been modified to support the story's clues, progression, and character development. These adaptations were made to enhance the fictional narrative while retaining the historical atmosphere.

This story includes a fictional *HMS Endeavour* during the period when Thomas and Edmund sailed. Although an *HMS Endeavour* famously captained by James Cook existed later, the *Endeavour* here does not reflect any specific historical vessel. Any resemblance to real ships or events is coincidental and supports the fictional narrative.

This novel was crafted with the support of ChatGPT, an AI tool developed by OpenAI. Its assistance in brainstorming, refining ideas, and polishing text was invaluable throughout the creative process.

Author, Editor & Cover Designer

Andrew Pang

Thank You for Choosing This Book!

If you enjoy reading *The Arch Scar,* please consider leaving a review on Amazon. Reviews from readers like you make a big difference by helping others discover the book and allowing me to keep creating stories.

How to Leave a Review:

- Visit your **Amazon** account.
- Select Returns & Orders.
- Find this **The Arch Scar** book from your orders.
- Select **Write a product review** and share your thoughts!

Thank you for your support—it means the world!

For my beloved sister, Lisa Ball.

Your spirit shines on in our hearts and memories.

Chapter 1

The rain tapped steadily against the window, a rhythmic reminder of the quiet tension in the room. The faint scent of old paper, leather-bound books, and forgotten history lingered, grounding them in the weight of the past. Daniel Grey sat at a weathered oak table, his fingers brushing over the edge of a faded envelope.

It wasn't just any envelope—this was a handmade enclosure, crafted with meticulous care. The thick paper bore faint creases from where it had been folded with precision, and the once-pristine wax seal was cracked and worn, a testament to the centuries it had endured. Daniel's historian instincts stirred; envelopes of this kind were rare in the early 18th century, often reserved for documents of exceptional importance. The deliberate craftsmanship suggested someone who valued both the letter's contents and its presentation.

Across from him, Sophie knelt beside a wooden chest, her hands shifting through piles of yellowed documents, maps, and ledgers. The chest's contents were a chaotic patchwork of history, but her movements slowed when she caught sight of Daniel's focused expression.

"This envelope alone tells a story," he murmured, more to himself than to Sophie, his voice tinged with awe. "Someone went to great lengths to protect what's inside."

"How long have these been sitting here?" Sophie asked, glancing up from the mess of papers. There was a mix of impatience and curiosity in her voice as she lifted a crumbling logbook, its pages barely holding together.

Daniel didn't answer immediately, his attention fixed on the envelope in his hands. "A long time," he murmured. "Too long."

Sophie set the logbook aside and looked at him. "We've gone through all this before. Do you really think we'll find anything new this time?"

Daniel remained silent, his thumb running absently along the edge of the envelope. This wasn't just another historical curiosity—it was a lifeline to a past he'd only read about in stories. His entire life had been dedicated to understanding the men who'd come before him, but this was different. This was his family's story, demanding to be heard. Daniel's gaze softened as he spoke. "History doesn't give up its secrets easily. Sometimes, you have to be ready to see what's been in front of you the whole time."

Daniel carefully opened the envelope, his movements deliberate. On the back of the parchment, an ornate "Z" caught his eye—a flourish reminiscent of medieval manuscripts. He paused briefly, taking in the detail, then unfolded the brittle sheet. As the parchment opened fully, its elegant 18th-century penmanship came into view. The ink, faded but legible, seemed to carry the weight of the writer's urgency through time. Daniel's pulse quickened as he began to read, each word drawing him closer to the past now laid bare in his hands.

"Lieutenant Edmund Grey," he murmured. "Addressed to his father... written just before his final voyage, months after the capture of La Fortuna."

Sophie sat up straighter, her eyes sharpening. "Edmund Grey? Our Edmund Grey?"

Daniel nodded slowly. "The very same. The family legend. The one everyone dismissed as a story."

The room seemed to close in around them, the rain outside tapping more insistently against the window. Sophie leaned forward, her curiosity now fully engaged.

"Let me see," she said, shifting closer.

Daniel angled the parchment to share, the faint script etched across its surface like the distant voice of its creator.

"Father," Daniel read aloud, his voice dropping as if the walls themselves were listening.

"15th August, 1708. We took the Spanish galleon, La Fortuna, in the Caribbean. Her holds brimmed with wealth, more than any of us could have imagined. The journey home has been long and fraught with danger—storms, enemy vessels, the constant threat of betrayal. Many good men were lost, far too many. If you are reading this, Father, it means that the sea has claimed me as well. But what we brought back, that which was fought for and won, still remains.

When path lost to the sea, look for the light that has guided our family through the storm. Beneath it lies the memory of the past, written in glass for all to see."

Sophie frowned, her eyes scanning the cryptic lines. "What does that mean?"

Daniel leaned back, his mind painting the picture of La Fortuna's long journey from the Caribbean. "It's a clue."

"A clue?" Sophie's scepticism was evident, but there was a spark of intrigue in her voice now. "To what?"

"The treasure," Daniel said quietly, his voice firm. "The one Edmund and his fellow officers took from the Spanish galleon La Fortuna. This letter... it's his way of telling his father where it's hidden."

Sophie's heart began to race. Treasure. The stories about the Grey family had always been a source of fascination, but no one had ever truly believed them. A lost fortune, stolen by naval officers and hidden away, never to be found—until now. It all seemed impossible, yet here it was, in black and white, etched onto a letter centuries old.

But for Sophie, this wasn't just about the thrill of finding treasure. Growing up, she had watched Daniel dedicate his life to studying the past, piecing together the fragmented history of their ancestors. And while she had always admired his passion, she'd never felt like it was something they shared—until now. This discovery was different. It was more than just a link to the past; it was a chance for Sophie to connect with her father on his own terms, to be a part of the legacy he had always tried to uncover.

"The journey home," Daniel began, his voice thoughtful, "wasn't a swift or easy return. The Caribbean in 1708 was perilous—pirates, storms, enemy ships at every turn. Navigating these waters was a deadly game. Any misstep could have meant disaster—not just from natural threats but also from the Spanish, who would stop at nothing to reclaim what had been taken from them. Disease could strike a crew at any moment. Edmund's letter makes it clear they faced constant danger—'storms, enemy vessels, and the constant threat of betrayal,' as he put it. They wouldn't have sailed straight home.

No, they would have been forced to dock in neutral ports, repair the ship, and perhaps even hide parts of what they had captured along the way. La Fortuna's fall was just the beginning—the real challenge was surviving the return with the prize still intact.

Sophie leaned forward, her attention caught. "So they survived the journey, but...?"

"But Edmund didn't make it much longer after that," Daniel replied. "This letter suggests that after their return, they were sent out again. Redeployed before they could enjoy their ill-gotten gains. The treasure was hidden, and the officers who knew about it... well, they didn't live long enough to retrieve it."

"Look for the light that has guided us through the storm," Sophie repeated, her mind working through the riddle. "That could be a lighthouse."

Daniel shook his head slowly. "No... it's something bigger than that. This is a place tied to our family, to the sea. A place with history, but also with a personal connection."

Sophie frowned, thinking through the possibilities. "So where is it?"

Daniel sat back, the answer slowly crystallising in his mind. "A harbour. A port where treasure-laden ships would return. Where officers like Edmund would have been stationed, where they could hide something... and know it would remain hidden."

Sophie's pulse quickened as the pieces began to fall into place. "A place tied to naval power, where treasure from ships like La Fortuna would have passed through. A stronghold."

Daniel's eyes lit up, the answer suddenly clear. Portsmouth. England's great naval heart. It had been the stronghold for centuries—where the greatest ships, officers, and admirals had passed through, a city forged by the sea and by history. It was the place where treasure-laden ships returned to port, where officers like Edmund would have been stationed. Its stone towers had seen the riches of nations flow through its harbour, its sea walls protecting the legacy of kings and queens.

"Portsmouth," he said quietly, his voice filled with certainty. "It's Portsmouth."

Sophie hesitated, not fully understanding the significance. "Portsmouth?" she repeated, a hint of confusion in her voice.

Daniel nodded, his excitement building. "Portsmouth Harbour. The heart of England's naval power. It makes perfect sense. The Grey family's history is tied to the sea and Portsmouth... it's been at the centre of that history for centuries."

Sophie's eyes widened, the pieces slowly falling into place. "So that's where we need to go," she said, her voice more certain now. "Portsmouth Harbour."

Daniel nodded. "The cathedral. It must be there. The light that has guided our family through the storm —it's got to be the windows. The stained glass."

Sophie felt the enormity of the revelation settle over her, the room suddenly seeming too small for everything they'd uncovered.

"Tomorrow," Daniel said, his voice calm but filled with purpose. "We go to Portsmouth."

Sophie met his gaze, the excitement now electric between them. The rain outside drummed harder as though the world itself were urging them forward.

"Portsmouth," Sophie whispered, the word now charged with meaning. "It all starts there."

Chapter 2

The train rattled steadily along the tracks, cutting through the green expanse of the countryside. Sophie leaned her head against the window, watching the rolling hills give way to industrial buildings and, finally, the distant shimmer of the sea. Sophie couldn't help but feel the growing anticipation in her chest as if the distant coast was pulling her toward something more than just another trip with her father. She found herself thinking of their family's stories, the way history always seemed to have them in its grasp. Was this journey about the treasure, or was it about something more personal? The air felt lighter the closer they got to the coast as if the promise of adventure hung just beyond the horizon.

Daniel sat opposite her, rifling through his notes and maps, though his gaze occasionally drifted out of the window, a smile tugging at the corners of his mouth. His mind wandered between the past and present, as if the historical maps before him and the landscape outside were somehow connected. As a historian, he knew this journey wasn't just a treasure hunt—it was a quest to uncover the Grey family's true legacy. The treasure was only part of the story, a fragment of something much more significant.

Sophie glanced down at her phone, her fingers gliding across the screen. Daniel noticed and raised an eyebrow, trying to hide his concern.

"Social media?" he asked, with a hint of disapproval. "You know, back in my day, we scrolled through books, not screens."

Sophie rolled her eyes but couldn't help a slight grin. "Back in your day, Dad, the only thing scrolling was the parchment."

Daniel sighed, assuming she was lost in the endless scroll of apps and updates. He turned back to his notes, trying to focus. Suddenly, he broke the silence. "Portsmouth is different. It isn't just a city by the sea." His tone carried the reverence of a historian. "This place has been at the heart of England's naval power for centuries. Every corner, every cobbled street, has witnessed history—battles won, ships launched, lives changed."

Sophie glanced up this time, slipping her phone into her pocket. "How so?"

Daniel explained. "It's a living relic, a place where centuries of naval history are still etched into the very landscape. You'll see. Portsmouth isn't just a harbour—it's a gateway to the past."

Sophie nodded, she had visited Portsmouth a few times but had never thought of it as anything more than a coastal city. The way her father spoke about it, though, made it sound like something out of a history book, a place where time hadn't entirely moved on.

As the train pulled into Portsmouth Harbour station, Sophie felt the distinct change in atmosphere. They stepped off the train and onto the wooden platform, the creak of the planks beneath their feet immediately setting the harbour apart from any other station. The platform extended out over the water, the salty tang of the sea in the air mixing with the cries of seagulls and the faint hum of the ferries docking nearby.

"This station is one of a kind." Daniel glanced around as he spoke. "Built on a pier, right over the water. Portsmouth

Harbour station is unique, but not entirely one of a kind. There are other stations like it—Hythe Pier and Lymington Pier, for example." His eyes swept over the wooden platform. "But Portsmouth... it's special. It's more than just a stop for commuters. For centuries, this has been a gateway for sailors returning from voyages, sometimes with riches, sometimes with nothing but their lives."

Sophie looked down, seeing the waves lapping gently against the wooden supports beneath them. The entire platform seemed to sway ever so slightly with the rhythm of the tide.

"It feels alive," she murmured, hearing the creaks and groans of the old wood beneath her feet.

"That's the sea talking to you," Daniel replied with a smile. "It's always moving, always shifting. Portsmouth Harbour has been a vital part of this city for centuries—ships coming and going, sailors setting off for war or returning home, and now us, following a trail that's hundreds of years old."

Sophie's phone buzzed in her pocket, but she ignored it, casting one last glance at the waves below before following her father.

As they moved towards the end of the platform, Sophie noticed the towering figure of a ship ahead of them. HMS Warrior stood in the harbour, its sleek black hull glistening in the daylight, its masts reaching up towards the sky.

"That's HMS Warrior." Daniel's posture straightened, his tone shifting to that of a seasoned historian. "Launched in 1860. She was the first iron-hulled warship ever built—faster and more heavily armed than anything else afloat at the time. She never saw combat, though. Just the threat of her was enough to keep enemies at bay."

Sophie gazed up at the ship, awed by its size and presence. "So, it was all just for show?"

"In a way, yes," Daniel replied. "But it worked. HMS Warrior was a symbol of Britain's naval power. No one wanted to face her, so she never had to fire a shot."

They walked past the ship, the sound of the harbour bustling around them. Ferries to the Isle of Wight came and went, and the distant clang of rigging against masts filled the air as sailors tended to smaller boats moored in the harbour.

Stepping off the pier, they made their way to an area just outside the station known as The Hard. The cobbled ground beneath their feet was rough and uneven, worn down by centuries of foot traffic. The modern world seemed to recede as Daniel gestured around them.

"This is The Hard," he said. "It was a landing platform for boats—a place where cargo would be unloaded and where people would come ashore. But there's more to it than that."

Sophie looked at him curiously. "More?"

Daniel nodded. "Back in the 19th century, when ships would dock here, there were boys known as mudlarks who would wait for low tide. They'd wade out into the mud, searching for pennies that people would throw into the muck. It was a tough life, scavenging for whatever they could find to survive."

Sophie frowned. "People threw coins into the mud on purpose?"

"Some did." Daniel nodded, his gaze distant as though picturing the scene. "It was almost a game for passersby, but for the mudlarks, it was serious work. They'd sift through the mud for hours, knee-deep in filth, hoping to find enough coins to eat for the day." Sophie's gaze drifted towards the harbour, imagining the boys, their hands black with mud, scouring the ground for any glint of copper or silver. The thought was sobering, a stark reminder of the harsh realities that lay beneath the grandeur of the sea and the ships.

"It's hard to believe how much history is buried here," Sophie murmured. "So many lives, so many stories, just washed away with the tide."

"Exactly." Daniel's tone was quiet but firm as he gazed around. "Portsmouth has seen everything—riches and poverty, war and peace. This place is built on the bones of the past, and the mudlarks were part of that story."

They stood for a moment, the sounds of the harbour fading into the background as Sophie absorbed the significance of the past coming to light.

Her phone buzzed again. She glanced at the screen, a small smile crossing her face, but this time she didn't respond. Daniel noticed and raised an eyebrow, his curiosity stirred.

"Come on." Daniel broke the silence at last, straightening his shoulders. "We've got a treasure of our own to find."

With the echo of history trailing behind them, they began walking towards the cathedral, the next step on their journey beckoning.

Chapter 3

The brisk wind from Portsmouth Harbour followed Daniel and Sophie as they approached Portsmouth Cathedral. The building loomed ahead, its pale stone exterior contrasting sharply with the overcast sky. The cathedral had been a steadfast presence in the city for centuries, surviving fires, wars, and the ravages of time. As they drew nearer, its weathered walls seemed to whisper stories of a thousand years of history.

Sophie's eyes were wide with wonder as they reached the cathedral. As they neared the imposing structure, Sophie felt an unexpected pull. It wasn't just the age or the architecture that struck her—it was the deep sense of history etched into every stone. the full meaning of their quest began to sink in, pressing on her as if the cathedral itself held the answers within its walls. "I've never actually been inside," she admitted. "I always expected it to be more grand, but... there's something about it. You can feel the history."

Daniel smiled, appreciating her enthusiasm. "It's not Westminster Abbey, but it's still rich with history. It's been rebuilt and expanded several times, often in the wake of destruction. The Great Fire of Portsmouth in 1680 ravaged parts of the city, and again during the Blitz of World War II, much of the cathedral had to be restored. But through all of this, the cathedral has stood as a symbol of resilience. That's what makes it interesting—you can see the layers of history as you walk through it."

They stepped inside, the heavy wooden doors creaking as they pushed them open. The interior greeted them with cool air and the soft scent of incense. Sunlight streamed through the tall windows, casting colourful reflections on the stone floor.

"The colours!" Sophie gasped, her voice soft but filled with wonder. "It's like the windows are painting the floor."

Daniel nodded, his eyes scanning the cathedral's nave. "Stained glass isn't just art—it's a message. In medieval times, these windows weren't just decorative; they told stories for people who couldn't read. That's why so many of them show biblical scenes. They're like windows into the past, into people's lives and beliefs. That's what's incredible about old churches—how the light and architecture work together to create an atmosphere. It draws you in."

They walked further in, past rows of pews, and Sophie found herself drawn to the stained glass windows that lined the walls. Some were simple, geometric patterns, but others depicted biblical scenes in vivid colours, their hues softened by time.

"Let's take a look at some of the windows," Daniel suggested, pointing toward the far side of the cathedral where some of the most renowned stained glass works were displayed. "The clues Edmund left in his letter said something about stained glass—maybe we'll find something that fits."

Sophie moved to the first window they came across. It was modern, its glass depicting an explosion of colours arranged in chaotic swirls. A small plaque beneath it noted that the window had been installed after World War II to honour those lost in the bombings.

"This one's modern," Sophie remarked. "Definitely not what we're looking for."

Daniel nodded. "No, but it's a beautiful piece of history in itself. The bombings during World War II were devastating for Portsmouth. Much of the city was rebuilt, but this window is a reminder of that time."

They moved along the row of windows, and Sophie's eyes widened when they came to a large, striking depiction of a ship rising from the water. "Wait, what about this?" she asked. "It's the Mary Rose."

Daniel stepped closer, examining the glass. The scene depicted the raising of the Mary Rose, Henry VIII's famous warship, which had sunk in the Solent during a naval battle and was salvaged centuries later.

"That's a recent window," Daniel said, shaking his head. "The Mary Rose was raised in the 1980s. Edmund's clue would have been left long before that."

Sophie sighed, deflated for a moment, but the sense of wonder remained in her voice. "It's amazing how much history is here. Even if it's not the right clue, it's hard not to get caught up in the stories these windows tell."

Daniel smiled, appreciating the way she was getting pulled into the moment. "That's what makes this place special. It's a collection of so many moments in time, all captured in glass."

They moved on, making their way toward a section of the cathedral that housed older stained glass windows. The colours in these were more muted, the images less clear, but there was a quiet strength to them that seemed to speak of endurance and faith.

Suddenly, Daniel stopped, his gaze fixed on one particular window. "There," he whispered, motioning to Sophie. "Look at that one."

Sophie stepped closer. This window was different from the others. It was smaller, less vibrant, but the image was unmistakable—Portsmouth Harbour, with small ships sailing through its waters. On the edge of the window stood a solitary tower, watching over the harbour like a guardian. Beneath the image, faint but visible, was an inscription in Latin.

"That's it," Daniel said softly, his heart racing. "This is the one."

Sophie frowned, her eyes tracing the lines of the inscription. "But it's in Latin. Can you read it?"

Daniel squinted, trying to decipher the text. "I can make out parts of it... something about ships and protection. But Latin's not my strongest skill."

Sophie grinned, reaching into her bag. "Hold on, I've got an app for that."

"Of course you do," Daniel chuckled, shaking his head.

She pulled out her phone and opened a translation app that used the camera to translate text in real time. She pointed it at the inscription, and after a moment, the words appeared on her screen.

"Per Dei voluntatem, naves nostrae insulam hanc beatam a procellis et hostibus custodiunt. Ubi turris naves custodit et portum protegit, robur regni nostri perseverat."

Sophie's eyes widened as the app translated the Latin: "By God's will, our ships guard this blessed isle from storms and foes. Where the tower watches over the ships and shields the harbour, the strength of our realm endures."

She looked up at Daniel, her heart racing. "That's part of the clue, isn't it? It matches a line from Edmund's letter!"

Sophie pulled the letter from her bag, carefully smoothing it out on the nearest bench.

Daniel's fingers brushed the delicate parchment, and for a moment, he could almost feel Edmund's presence—this long-dead relative who had set all of this in motion. It was as if time had collapsed, and the distance between them, between centuries, had narrowed. His eyes scanned the familiar lines until they rested on the passage:

"When path lost to the sea, look for the light that has guided our family through the storm. Beneath it lies the memory of the past, written in glass for all to see."

Daniel continued, his voice quiet with excitement. "By God's will, our ships guard this blessed isle from storms and foes."

Sophie's breath caught in her throat. "It's the same. This is definitely the clue." She paused, her gaze lingering on the bench where the letter lay. "I've always known about our family's naval history, but standing here, seeing it written in this letter... it feels like I'm part of something much bigger, like we're walking in their footsteps."

Daniel nodded, but his focus was on the second part of the inscription. "But what about the rest? *'Where the tower watches over the ships and shields the harbour...'*"

Sophie quickly looked back at her phone and read aloud the translation. "Where the tower watches over the ships and shields the harbour, the strength of our realm endures."

She glanced at Daniel, her gaze intent as she considered. "Does this mean there's another clue connected to a tower?"

Daniel's eyes widened slightly, a flicker of recognition crossing his face. "The tower... that must be the watchtower. It has to be a reference to The Round Tower."

He stepped closer to the window, his finger tracing the outline of a tower depicted in the stained glass. "Look here," he said, pointing to the lower section of the window. "This is the harbour, and right here... that's The Round Tower. You can see it standing over the ships, guarding the entrance."

Sophie leaned in, her eyes following his gesture, and sure enough, there was the unmistakable image of The Round Tower, as seen from the harbour. Its stone structure rose solidly from the shore, a watchful guardian over the water. The depiction in the glass was both elegant and subtle, blending into the scene of ships and the bustling harbour below.

"The Round Tower... Is it important? I've heard of it, but I'm not really sure about its history," Sophie asked, her curiosity growing.

Daniel nodded, his mind racing. "Exactly. The Round Tower has been standing there since the 15th century, guarding the harbour and the ships that came through. Edmund must have been familiar with it. The letter..." He trailed off, tapping the glass gently. "He was pointing us here, to this very window, to guide us to the next clue."

Sophie took a step back, a grin spreading across her face. "So, the watchtower in the stained glass... that must be The Round Tower. That's where we're headed next, right?" She felt a thrill run through her. They were standing on the edge of a secret, a treasure hunt that had lain dormant for centuries. The world outside seemed to fade, the sounds of the bustling harbour a distant hum. This was real, and they were getting closer."

Daniel's heart pounded as the realization settled in. "Yes," he said with a quiet conviction, "The Round Tower is our next destination."

Sophie, her fingers still lingering over the parchment, slowly folded it, careful as if handling a sacred relic. She placed it back into her bag, her mind already racing with the possibilities of what lay ahead.

Daniel straightened, his eyes gleaming with purpose. "We're close, Sophie. So close." His voice was taut with anticipation, a thrill echoing in every syllable.

Sophie felt it too, that surge of excitement that left her pulse quickening. They were no longer spectators of history, but participants in an ancient riddle. The next step in their journey was imminent, and as they stood on the threshold of discovery, neither of them could imagine what awaited.

Chapter 4

The thick mud sucked at her boots with each step, the cold water lapping just below her knees. Her nylon fishing waders clung tightly to her legs, coated in a film of mud that had long since become a part of the landscape. The wind cut across the open creek, sharp and biting, but she paid it no mind. Her focus was on the small screen in her hand, where the drone she controlled buzzed steadily overhead.

She gritted her teeth as the drone dipped low over the mud. Every muscle in her body tensed with a focus that bordered on obsession. Failure wasn't an option—though she wouldn't admit it, even to herself.

The remote steady in her grasp as she manoeuvred the drone over the marshland, its camera capturing every shift and dip in the terrain below. She stood alone, knee-deep in the creek, her hood pulled low over her face, shielding her from the elements. A thin ponytail peeked out from beneath the hood, her hair damp from the mist that hung over the water like a veil.

She was dressed for this. The mud, the cold, the relentless wind—it was all part of the job. The nylon waders kept her dry, but they did little to shield her from the biting chill that crawled up her legs. Her weatherproof coat, zipped up to her chin, and gloves protected her hands from the icy air. Despite the

And now here she was. Fareham Creek—an isolated stretch of muddy water and forgotten land, where the sea whispered secrets to those who cared enough to listen.

Her drone hovered over the bank, its camera locked on the disturbance below. She leaned forward, staring at the screen as the feed zoomed in on the faint glimmer beneath the mud. Something metallic. A structure, perhaps? A hidden chamber? Her heart raced at the thought.

"When the sea turns to land and the tides no longer call, seek where time has swallowed the truth." The words came unbidden, the passage from her letter looping endlessly in her mind. She had spent months deciphering the letter's meaning, breaking it down, piece by maddening piece. Each line had brought her closer, each clue a step nearer to the truth.

Her eyes remained glued to the screen, her fingers tightening on the controls. Could this be it? The final piece? The answer she had been chasing for what felt like an eternity.

She breathed out slowly, forcing herself to stay calm. It was too soon to be sure, too dangerous to jump to conclusions. But the clues... they had led her here. The letter had spoken of a place where the water and land intertwined, where the past had sunk into the present. And Fareham Creek, with its winding, treacherous tides and muddy banks, had fit the description perfectly.

Her boots shifted in the mud as she adjusted the drone's position, the camera sweeping over the banks one last time. The metallic glint below was more visible now, teasing her with the promise of discovery.

She wasn't ready to move just yet. Not until she was sure. The mud held its secrets tightly, and one wrong step could undo everything. She needed more evidence, more certainty. But the nagging sensation that she was on the edge of something monumental was growing with every passing second.

Suddenly, a sharp buzz in her coat pocket jolted her focus. Her phone. She grit her teeth, a flicker of irritation flashing across her face. She hesitated, her breath held in the tense moment. Not now.

The phone buzzed again, more insistent. Forcing herself to exhale, Claire reached for the device. Her eyes never left the screen, still locked on the metallic glimmer in the mud as she fished the phone from her pocket. She glanced down quickly—just long enough to see the message. Her pulse quickened. The timing couldn't have been worse.

She slipped the phone back into her pocket, forcing herself to block out the distraction. There would be time for that later, once she was sure of what she'd found. She adjusted the drone, guiding it even closer to the shimmering object buried beneath the surface. The wind howled through the reeds, the cold pressing harder against her, but she stayed locked in position.

The metal was more visible now, sharper—almost within reach.

The buzzing of her phone faded from her mind as the thrill of discovery pulsed through her.

So close.

Chapter 5

15th August 1708 – The Caribbean Sea.

The humidity clung to Lieutenant Edmund Grey like the sweat of battle, the air heavy with the scent of salt and gunpowder. The ship beneath him, the once-proud Spanish galleon La Fortuna, now lay battered and bloodied, its Spanish crew defeated. The Union Jack fluttered above the mast, tattered from the skirmish, while the British sailors worked below deck, taking stock of their spoils.

Edmund gripped the weathered railing, staring into the endless blue of the Caribbean. The swell of the water was calm. His thoughts, anything but. Victory should have tasted sweeter, but his mind was on the treasure below—the fortune in gold and silver that could rival the Crown's.

He felt the pull of duty, a heavy sense of loyalty tugging at his conscience, with each oath sworn to the Crown clashing against his responsibility to his family—the future they deserved. Could he sacrifice one to save the other? His mind raced, caught in a storm of conflicting loyalties, but one thing was clear—he couldn't let the Crown take it all.

Footsteps echoed across the deck. Captain Thomas Hastings, the ship's commander, approached—his presence as sharp as his calculating gaze. Thomas had seen battle after battle, and Edmund knew he was more than just an officer; he was a strategist. As the captain stood next to him, their eyes were not on the horizon, but on the spoils won below deck.

"It's a king's ransom down there." Thomas leaned in slightly, his voice low and almost conspiratorial. "Enough to buy ships of our own, Edmund."

Edmund didn't respond immediately. His thoughts remained anchored to the gravity of what lay in the hold. "The Crown will take its share," he muttered, the bitterness in his voice unmistakable.

Thomas grunted, his jaw tightening. "Aye, and leave us with the scraps, as they always do. Men like us, who bleed and sweat for these riches, end up with nothing more than a few pounds to our names."

Edmund turned to face him, the decision forming like the tightening of a sailor's knot. "Not this time, Thomas."

The captain narrowed his eyes, a flicker of understanding passing between them. "What are you saying, Edmund?"

"I'm saying we keep some," Edmund replied, his voice firm. "The Crown will have its cut, but not all of it. We've earned more than that—our men have earned more than that." He paused, the sea breeze rustling his coat. "We hide our share. Keep it safe. For our families. For the future."

Thomas glanced over his shoulder, scanning the deck for any prying ears. His voice dropped to a whisper. "You're talking about stealing from the Crown. That's treason."

"It's not treason if no one knows," Edmund shot back. "We take enough to secure our families, to make sure all of this—" he gestured to the blood-streaked deck, the fallen men, the cannon damage "—wasn't for nothing."

for them—it would be for the future. For those who would come after them.

The wind picked up, carrying the scent of the coming storm. Edmund stared at the vast horizon. There was no turning back now. The treasure's future—and his family's—was sealed beneath layers of secrecy. One wrong move, and the consequences could be deadly.

The treasure of *La Fortuna* would not be the Crown's reward. It would be their legacy.

Chapter 6

The walk to The Round Tower was short, only a few minutes from the heart of the city, but the combination of ancient stone buildings and modern constructions caught Sophie's attention almost immediately.

Sophie glanced around, intrigued by the unusual blend of history and modernity in the streets. "Isn't it strange?" she said, breaking the silence. "The way these really old buildings are standing right next to modern ones? It feels... disjointed."

Daniel slowed his pace, nodding thoughtfully. "It is, but there's a reason for it. Portsmouth was one of the most heavily bombed cities in the UK during World War II. Much of the city was destroyed, and what survived was rebuilt right alongside what was left. The Luftwaffe focused on the dockyards and the naval base. It's a city rebuilt from its own rubble, standing alongside its past."

Sophie's eyes lingered on a section of the street where a sleek, glass-fronted building stood next to a centuries-old stone wall. "So, a lot of what we're seeing was rebuilt after the war?"

Daniel nodded. "Exactly. What survived bears the imprint of history, and what was rebuilt reflects resilience. The scars of war are still there, though softened with time. It's a mix of different eras—some buildings date back centuries, while others were hastily constructed in the post-war years."

Sophie absorbed the explanation, her gaze following the line of rooftops leading toward the harbour. "It's like the city wears its history on the outside—scars and all."

Daniel smiled softly at that. "A perfect way to describe it."

As they continued walking, Sophie's eyes narrowed, a teasing grin spreading across her face. "Have you noticed how many pubs we've passed in just a few minutes?" she quipped, breaking the solemn tone.

Daniel chuckled. "That's another part of Portsmouth's history. It's a sailor's city through and through. You'll find pubs on nearly every corner, especially around here. Back in the day, they were filled with sailors fresh from the sea, spending their pay, and trading stories—some more real than others."

Sophie looked at the old pub signs, faded but still defiant against time. "So, these places are as much a part of the city's history as the buildings themselves?"

"Absolutely," Daniel replied. "Some of them have been around for centuries. They were places where sailors and merchants did business, where deals were made, and where a lot of history was forged over a pint or two."

As they neared The Round Tower, Sophie's attention was drawn to something unexpected. Built into the fortress walls of the old structure were rows of artist studios, nestled into what was now called Hotwalls Studios. Local artists had transformed the ancient military stronghold into creative spaces, their colourful works displayed within the once-formidable walls.

"This is... amazing," Sophie paused, taking in the contrast. "All these artists working here, inside an old fortress. It's hard to believe this place used to be all about defence."

Daniel nodded, his voice taking on a more thoughtful tone. "That's Portsmouth for you. It's always been a city of reinvention. The Round Tower was built in the 15th century as part of a network of coastal defences. This whole area was once a vital part of the city's military strength. But now, artists and creativity have replaced cannons and soldiers. It's history being reimagined, repurposed."

Sophie turned her gaze to the tower itself. The thick, weathered stone walls rose up before them, dominating the harbour, a silent witness to centuries of conflict and change. The fortress had stood here for more than 500 years, watching over the sea, protecting Portsmouth from invaders.

"It's incredible that it's still standing after all these years," Sophie craned her neck to take in the sheer size of the structure.

Daniel smiled. "It's seen a lot of history. Wars, invasions, even the bombings during World War II. But through it all, it's stood firm. And now, it might be holding our next clue."

The open space around the tower connected directly with the Hotwalls walkway, allowing visitors to stroll freely between the tower and the studios. A gentle breeze swept through, and the sound of waves lapping against the nearby shore filled the air. Sophie took it all in, realising that they were standing in a place where countless soldiers and sailors had once watched and waited, protecting their city.

hunting for the clue Thomas had hinted at: *'where the light would guide you.'* She had never found anything. Were Daniel and Sophie seeing something she had missed?

"What did they find?" she asked, the edge in her voice more pronounced now.

The man shook his head. "If they found anything, they didn't show it."

Claire's frustration simmered just beneath the surface. She had scoured every inch of that cathedral. The clues had led her nowhere—yet. There was always the chance that Daniel and Sophie held the key that had eluded her for so long. The possibility clawed at her, stoking the fire of impatience.

"They've been at it for hours," the man continued, his voice cutting through her thoughts. "If they've found something, they're keeping it to themselves."

She clenched her jaw. "Where are they now?"

His response was calm, measured. "The Round Tower. That's where they've gone."

The words struck her like a sharp gust of wind. Claire's thoughts spun—she had spent countless hours at The Round Tower, poring over every detail, every mark etched into the stone. But she had found nothing concrete, only faint echoes of a past too far buried. Now, it seemed like Daniel was about to discover something she couldn't.

Her fingers itched to clutch the letter from Thomas again, to pore over its lines in the hope that it would reveal something— anything—before it was too late. But she had read those lines a hundred times; they wouldn't change. She had already spent months on this puzzle, and the pieces simply didn't fit.

Maybe, just maybe, Daniel and Sophie would find what she could not. Or maybe they, too, would come up empty-handed, leaving Claire no closer to her goal.

She stood abruptly, her coat sweeping around her as she turned toward the door. The man remained seated, his presence a quiet reminder that she was not the only one invested in the outcome of this search.

"Keep following them," Claire ordered, her voice low but firm. "And tell me the moment they make their next move."

With that, she swept out of the cathedral, her mind already racing with possibilities. She couldn't afford to let anyone else get ahead.

Chapter 8

"This place has seen everything." Daniel's voice was quiet as he gazed around. "And now, we're standing where they once stood, looking for our own answers."

Sophie gave one last glance at the artist studios tucked within the walls before turning her full attention to the tower. The history they were about to uncover felt closer than ever.

As they continued their exploration of The Round Tower, Sophie grew increasingly eager to find the clue mentioned in Edmund's letter. Her eyes scanned the area, taking in the weathered stones, the ancient walls, and the relics scattered around the tower's base. There was history here—so much of it. But where was the clue?

Her gaze fell on something large and rusted: a few massive iron links, remnants of what was once part of the Harbour Chain. The chain itself was long gone, but these remaining links were laid out on the courtyard floor, on display as a reminder of Portsmouth's defensive past. Sophie moved closer, inspecting the relic, and then called over her shoulder to Daniel.

"Look at this." She gestured toward the massive iron links, her eyes scanning them intently. "Do you think this ties into Edmund's clue?

Daniel joined her, his eyes following the line of the heavy iron links. "That's part of the Harbour Chain," A subtle smile crept onto his lips. "In the past, it was used to block enemy ships from entering the harbour. During times of war, the chain would be stretched across the mouth of the harbour, preventing any hostile vessels from getting through. But this," he gestured to the relic, "is just a remnant. The chain is long gone, and it's not connected to the tower itself. The chain was part of the naval defences, but its purpose was tactical. It doesn't fit the kind of clue Edmund would have left."

Sophie frowned, still staring at the heavy iron links. "But it's right here, and it's such a prominent feature of the harbour's defences. Maybe it represents the place where the tower meets the sea?"

Daniel shook his head. "It's a good thought, but the Harbour Chain was more of a deterrent than anything symbolic. Edmund would have been more deliberate in choosing his clues. He wouldn't have used something that was merely functional."

Sophie sighed, stepping back from the relic. She knew her father was probably right, but it was frustrating to come up empty-handed. "All right, then. What about the cannons?"

She moved toward the cannons lined up along the wall, their iron barrels rusted from centuries of exposure to the sea air. They were relics of a bygone era, their muzzles aimed out toward the harbour as if still ready to defend against an invasion.

"Edmund's ship would've had cannons like these, right?" Sophie tilted her head, studying the rough, weathered metal. "Maybe there's something here—some connection between the cannons on the ship and the ones used to defend the city."

Daniel followed her, shaking his head slightly. "You're not wrong that Edmund would have been familiar with cannons like these, but these particular guns were part of the tower's defence. They were stationed here to protect the harbour from attacks by sea. Cannons were essential in naval warfare, yes, but they're not part of Edmund's personal history in the way his clues would be."

He knelt beside one of the cannons, his fingers tracing the faint markings still visible on the surface. "These cannons date back to the 18th century, long after Edmund's time. The tower was retrofitted with new guns to keep up with advances in naval warfare. The ones Edmund would have known on his ship would've been smaller, less advanced than these."

Sophie watched as he examined the cannon, appreciating his depth of knowledge but still feeling the impatience bubbling inside her. "So, nothing here either?"

Daniel straightened up, dusting off his hands. "Nothing here, I'm afraid. The cannons are important in Portsmouth's military history, but they're not part of this particular puzzle. Edmund wouldn't have left something as general as this. His clue is specific, tied to his family and his legacy."

He paused for a moment, a grin spreading across his face. "Well, that's a *blast* from the past."

Sophie rolled her eyes, though a smile tugged at the corners of her mouth. "Dad, that was... cannon-ly terrible."

They both chuckled, the brief levity a welcome distraction from their otherwise frustrating search. Still, Sophie's gaze wandered back to the relics, as though hoping something would finally stand out.

As they moved further along the tower, Sophie's eyes caught something else—an obvious doorway, clearly leading to the inner sections of the tower, a place they hadn't explored yet. She hesitated, her fingers brushing the cold stone as a prickling sensation crawled up her spine. It was faint, but the feeling of being watched clung to her thoughts, prodding at the edges of her focus. She turned her head slightly, casting a glance over her shoulder, but the courtyard lay silent. Shaking off the unease, she pointed toward the entrance. "What about in there? Maybe there's something inside the tower itself."

Daniel followed her gaze toward the doorway, his expression tightening. A flicker of unease crossed his face, as though unseen eyes were tracking their every move. "We don't have access to the inner parts of the tower," he admitted, his tone measured. "It's closed off for now."

Sophie's shoulders dropped slightly in disappointment. "So, we can't get in?"

"Not without permission," Daniel replied. "We'd need to apply for access through the proper channels. But for now, we'll have to explore what we can on the outside. If we don't find what we're looking for, then we'll go through the process to get inside."

Sophie nodded, though the thought of potentially missing out on something important nagged at her. Still, Daniel was right—they needed to cover everything they could here first.

"Let's keep going." Daniel gestured toward the rest of the tower's exterior, his eyes scanning the stonework. "We might find something hidden around the foundation. If not, we'll come back for the rest."

They turned away from the obvious entrance, the wind carrying the sound of the sea up toward them as they prepared to continue their search.

After a thorough but unsuccessful search of the courtyard, Daniel and Sophie decided to make their way up the narrow stone steps leading to the top of The Round Tower. The climb was steep, the air cool and crisp, carrying the fresh scent of the sea. When they finally emerged onto the tower's upper platform, they were greeted by a sweeping view that stretched across Portsmouth Harbour and beyond.

Sophie paused, her breath catching, not solely from the climb but from the awe-inspiring scene before her. The harbour waters gleamed under the pale sky, reflecting the bobbing masts of the ships docked below. In the distance, the rugged outline of the Isle of Wight stood against the horizon, while the Solent Forts—man-made islands—dotted the sea.

"Wow," Sophie murmured, leaning against the stone wall and looking out over the vast expanse of water. "Just imagine how many ships would have passed through here over the centuries. All those sailors coming and going, like Edmund."

Daniel stepped beside her, nodding. "Hundreds... maybe thousands, even hundreds of thousands." His voice was steady as he glanced toward the harbour. "This place has been a hub of activity for centuries, and The Round Tower was crucial to its defence. Sailors would have stood exactly where we are now, scanning for signs of approaching threats—enemy ships, pirates, even the Spanish Armada at one point."

His eyes shifted to the harbour's horizon before he gestured toward the unmistakable outline of HMS Queen Elizabeth, the largest and most formidable aircraft carrier in the British Navy. "There she is—HMS Queen Elizabeth." She's a symbol of how far the Royal Navy has come. Commissioned in 2017, she's one of the most advanced warships in the world, carrying state-of-the-art F-35 fighter jets. A true floating airbase."

Sophie looked toward the carrier in awe. "She's massive."

Daniel smiled. "Nearly 65,000 tonnes, and over 280 metres long. Imagine the contrast to ships like Edmund's or even Nelson's *HMS Victory*. Back then, it was all about the number of cannons and the speed of the wind in your sails. Now it's radar systems, stealth aircraft, and nuclear submarines supporting from below. The way we defend this harbour has changed, but the principle remains the same—power and protection."

Sophie grinned and gestured toward the horizon again. "Isn't her sister ship called HMS *Prince of Wales*?"

"Yes," Daniel nodded. "Both carriers form the heart of the UK's Carrier Strike Group."

Sophie tilted her head, her voice playful. "Shouldn't they rename her *King Charles* by now? And if it's named after him, shouldn't it be a *son* ship of *Queen Elizabeth*?" She raised her eyebrows, teasing.

Daniel chuckled, catching on to her tone. "You know that's not how it works. Ships aren't named after current monarchs or based on family ties. They often carry historic names tied to the Royal Navy's legacy. HMS *Prince of Wales* was named after a long line of ships with that name dating back centuries."

Sophie smirked, already knowing the answer. "Yeah, I know. Just seeing if you'd go into professor mode again."

Sophie gazed out at the scene, picturing the tower in its heyday, bristling with cannons and soldiers scanning the horizon for danger. Ships, like Edmund Grey's, would have sailed through these very waters, carrying cargo, passengers, and, in some cases, treasure. But now, standing here centuries later, it was ships like the *Queen Elizabeth* that guarded these same waters, a testament to the Royal Navy's enduring presence.

But something felt off. Sophie turned to take in her surroundings. The top of the tower wasn't the ancient stronghold she had imagined. Instead, it had been transformed with benches arranged in neat rows, a designated viewing area for tourists eager to admire the harbour below. The smooth, polished wood of the seating felt at odds with the weathered stone, a modern touch that subtly altered the atmosphere.

"It's different than I thought it would be," Sophie remarked, eyeing the seating arrangement. "It's almost too... modern."

Daniel nodded, his expression thoughtful. "The top of the tower was rebuilt during the Napoleonic Wars. Between 1847 and 1850, they modified the roof to serve as a gun platform. It was meant to defend against new threats from the sea. And now..." He gestured to the benches and the modern touches. "Now it's a viewing platform for visitors. History layered on history."

Sophie's gaze shifted to the ground beneath her feet, noticing a dark, tar-like substance that spread across the roof. "What's this?" she asked, crouching down to inspect the weatherproofing material.

Daniel sighed. "That's the tar they used to weatherproof the roof. It's been here for a long time. Covers everything. If there were any clues or inscriptions etched into the stone... well, they'd be hidden under this now."

Sophie frowned. "So, even if Edmund left something here, it's been sealed up?"

"Possibly," Daniel admitted. "This modification was done after Edmund's time. It's likely anything that was here was covered when they repurposed the tower as a gun platform. Any carvings or marks he might have made would be under this layer."

The frustration was clear on Sophie's face. "So, that means we won't find anything up here?"

Daniel leaned against the wall, looking out at the horizon. "It's hard to say. The view is incredible, but it doesn't feel like the answer is here. If Edmund left a clue, it's likely somewhere less obvious. Something that hasn't been altered by modern hands."

They stood in silence for a moment, taking in the stunning view of the harbour. The ships moved slowly through the water, some heading out to sea, others returning to port. It was easy to get lost in the beauty and history of the scene, but the significance of their search weighed heavily on them.

"This doesn't make sense," she said abruptly, turning toward her father. "If this tower was a naval defence, a place meant to guard the city from invaders, how could Edmund expect his father to come here and find the clues he left? Wouldn't this place have been crawling with soldiers? It feels too risky."

Daniel paused in his own search, her question hanging in the air. He glanced at the tower, its stone walls etched with centuries of history. "You're right," considering her point. "On the surface, it doesn't seem like the ideal place to hide something. But maybe we're looking at it from the wrong perspective."

them. The elevated view hadn't revealed anything new, only adding to their growing questions. Emerging onto the ramparts, the sound of the waves below grew louder, their rhythmic crash a reminder of time's relentless passage.

As they approached the doorway leading to the tower's exterior, Sophie's pace slowed, her eyes catching on the cool, stone walls. She paused, examining faint lines carved into the stone, marks that seemed to crisscross and overlap through the years. At first glance, they looked like random scratches, but as she studied them, distinct patterns emerged—layers of graffiti from different eras.

"Look at this," she murmured, stepping closer to inspect the engravings. Some were the expected scrawls of visitors—Gaz was here boldly scratched next to a crude heart enclosing the initials J + M. Other marks were rougher, older. They seemed scratched in hurriedly, like messages left by soldiers long forgotten, stationed here to guard the coast. Their shapes were worn and indistinct, but one symbol caught her attention—a faint initial, almost hidden beneath layers of newer graffiti.

It was carefully inscribed, unlike the more casual scrawls surrounding it. A chill of anticipation ran through her as she examined it, her heart beginning to race. This mark didn't fit the rest; it felt deliberate, purposeful. She leaned closer, a flicker of excitement rising. Could this be the clue they'd been searching for all along?

Daniel stepped beside her, his gaze sweeping over the etchings. "A mixture of history," he said softly, "layered on top of each other, like the city itself."

Sophie nodded, continuing her inspection. Her attention shifted from one carving to another until something unusual caught her eye—a letter carved deeper than the others. It was faded, its edges worn by time, but unmistakable.

"Look at this one." Sophie leaned closer, gesturing toward the mark. "It's different from the rest."

Daniel leaned in, squinting at the carving. It was the letter 'G,' weathered and eroded by years of exposure. But what made it stand out was its resemblance to the way Edmund Grey signed his name—a deliberate, curved mark, simple yet distinctive.

"Could this be it?" Sophie asked, her voice low with anticipation.

Daniel's eyes narrowed as he studied the letter. "It's possible," he said, his tone cautious. "It's the right shape, and it's been here a long time."

But there was nothing else. No additional message, no symbol to confirm its significance. It was just a worn letter, carved into the stone like so many others.

They stood in silence for a moment, the importance of their search looming between them. The quiet stretched, an almost oppressive stillness settling over them. Sophie couldn't shake the feeling that someone was nearby, watching their every move. Yet when she glanced around again, the courtyard remained empty. Still, the unease lingered.

Then, almost as if to himself, Daniel began repeating the words of the clue, his voice barely more than a murmur.

"Where the watchtower meets the sea, written in glass for all to see."

Sophie glanced at him, intrigued by the sudden intensity in his voice. "What are you thinking?"

Daniel didn't answer immediately. He continued to repeat the phrase, his gaze narrowing in concentration. "Where the watchtower meets the sea, written in glass for all to see." He paused, his eyes flicking back to the Round Tower and then to the sea beyond.

"We've been interpreting it too abstractly," He turned to face her, a thoughtful expression crossing his face. "We've been thinking of this clue symbolically, like something hidden in a metaphor."

Sophie tilted her head, trying to follow his train of thought. "So what are you saying?"

Daniel's eyes were alight with sudden realisation. "What if it's literal?" his voice carried a growing excitement as he spoke. "What if Edmund meant exactly what he wrote? Where the watchtower meets the sea... what if that's not a metaphor at all? What if it's telling us to look at the base of the tower, where it physically meets the sea?"

Sophie's heart quickened. It made sense, in a way that none of their previous ideas had. The clue had been right in front of them, but they had been overthinking it, looking for something more hidden than it needed to be.

"The base of the tower..." Sophie repeated, her voice trailing off as her mind raced. "Do you think he left something there? A mark, a message?"

"It's the most logical place," Daniel's expression hardened with determination. "If he wanted to hide something, something only someone who knew the clues would find, the base of the tower would be perfect. It's where the tower literally meets the sea."

They both stood still for a moment, the reality of what they might be about to discover settling over them. The wind swept the salty tang of the sea toward them as the waves crashed ceaselessly against the stone walls below.

"Let's check it out," Sophie said, her voice filled with determination. Without another word, they headed for the base of the tower, ready to uncover what had been hidden for centuries.

With renewed focus, Daniel and Sophie made their way cautiously toward the base of The Round Tower. The path ahead was far from simple—the only access to the sea-facing side of the tower involved scaling a high stone wall, followed by navigating a treacherous descent over large sea defence boulders. The stones were slick with algae, and the sound of the rising tide crashing against the rocks below made the danger clear.

"This isn't exactly the safest route," Sophie muttered as she gripped the edge of the wall, carefully lowering herself down the other side. Her boots skidded slightly on the uneven surface of the boulders, but she steadied herself, her pulse quickening with the thrill of the hunt.

Daniel followed close behind, his movements careful but deliberate. His breath came short from the climb, but his resolve was clear. "Edmund wouldn't have left a clue that was easy to find. He would've ensured that anyone seeking it had to be just as determined as he was."

Once they were safely down, they found themselves on the sloping foundations at the very base of the tower. The stones here were worn smooth by centuries of pounding waves, and slick with algae and seaweed. Every step felt precarious, but neither of them was willing to turn back now. The tide was creeping closer, lapping at their feet, making their search more urgent.

"Look over there." Sophie pointed to a section where the seaweed clung densely to the stones. She crouched down, sweeping away the debris with steady movements. Beneath the seaweed, pebbles, and muck, faint carvings began to emerge on the stone.

Daniel knelt beside her, his heart pounding as they worked together to clear the debris. Slowly, something began to emerge from beneath the muck—a faint carving in the stone, worn by time but still visible.

Sophie paused, her breath catching as she swept away the last of the seaweed. "It's another 'G'," she whispered, her voice filled with awe. The familiar letter stood out, etched carefully, as if left as a sign.

Daniel's eyes widened. "Another one," he echoed, the realization of the discovery settling deep within him. They had found a 'G' before—could this be part of a deliberate trail, left by Edmund Grey?

Their hands stilled as the inscription beneath the 'G' slowly revealed itself. The words were faint but legible, as though waiting to be uncovered for centuries:

"To the fortress by the sea, where the king stood watch."

Daniel stared at the words, his heart racing. He glanced at Sophie, his voice steady but urgent. "Southsea Castle. This points to Henry VIII's fort. It was built to defend Portsmouth from invasion. Edmund must have hidden the next clue there."

As the waves lapped higher, Sophie stood, her eyes wide with excitement. "So that's where we go next?"

"Yes," Daniel confirmed, wiping his damp hands on his trousers. "We need to get to Southsea Castle before the trail... gets even colder."

Sophie smirked, catching on. "So it's the trail that's cold, or are you just freezing, Dad?"

But as they prepared to climb back up, Sophie felt it again—an inexplicable sense of being watched, of time running out. And then, the soft hum of a drone reached their ears, faint but unmistakable. Sophie looked up sharply. "Did you hear that?"

The drone hovered overhead, its camera trained on them, an intrusive observer to their discovery.

They turned instinctively toward the source of the noise. Standing a short distance away, on the pebble beach around the other side of the tower, was a woman. She was dressed in mud-splattered wading trousers, clearly made for tougher terrain, the kind used for navigating rivers and marshes. Her fitted jacket and practical boots suggested she was prepared for a long day of scouting. Her hair, damp from the sea air, was pulled back into a ponytail, and her sharp gaze remained fixed on them, assessing every move.

The tide had already closed off the beach access from where she stood, but she didn't seem concerned. The drone hovered above her, circling slowly, as if to ensure that no movement went unnoticed.

Daniel frowned, a sense of unease prickling at the back of his mind. "We're being watched."

Sophie nodded, her pulse quickening with the realisation. "She's been following us."

"Let's go," Daniel gestured for Sophie to follow, keeping his voice calm but urgent. "We've found the clue—we don't need to stick around for questions."

As they carefully made their way back up the treacherous boulders, Sophie couldn't help but glance back at the woman. She had never seen her before, but something about her felt deliberate. Whoever she was, she wasn't just an onlooker. And the fact that she was here now, watching them so intently, suggested that their search for the treasure had just become a lot more complicated.

The rising tide lapped at their feet as they hurried back toward safety, leaving behind the woman with her drone, her eyes still following their every move.

Chapter 9

17th August 1708 – The Caribbean Sea.

The warship creaked softly as it swayed with the gentle Caribbean current, the sound a constant companion to those who sailed her. In the dimly lit cabin, the air clung with humidity, sweat, and the unspoken tension surrounding Lieutenant Edmund Grey and Captain Thomas Hastings as they faced their decision.

The two men sat close, their shared silence heavy with trust and understanding. They had been through countless battles together, each one forging an unbreakable bond. To outsiders, Thomas was the captain, and Edmund the subordinate, but between the two of them, they were brothers. War had carved that bond deep, with every battle marking them in ways that went far beyond rank. They had saved each other's lives more times than either could count, and tonight, they were bound by something even greater—a secret that would test the strength of that bond.

Between them sat an iron-bound chest, its contents gleaming under the flickering light of the ship's lantern. Gold coins, silver ingots, and priceless Spanish artefacts lay within. The sway of the ship seemed to grow more pronounced, as if the treasure itself was dragging them deeper into the murky waters of doubt.

Thomas tapped the lid of the chest with a gloved hand, his weathered face calm but resolute. His voice, low and gravelled from years at sea, carried the weight of his decision. "We take this for ourselves. The Crown will claim the rest, but this... this is ours."

Edmund, sitting across from him, met his captain's gaze. The silence stretched between them, yet it wasn't awkward. It was trust—unspoken and solid. Still, beneath the calm surface, a ripple of doubt stirred within him. Were they betraying their oaths to the Crown, or securing a future their families deserved? "And if we don't make it back," he added, his voice a touch heavier now, "our families will know where to find it."

Yet even as the words left his mouth, a brief flicker of doubt unsettled Edmund. If the plan failed... what then? Was this betrayal, or simply survival? He clenched his fists, pushing the thought aside.

Thomas gave a slow nod. "Aye. If we survive this next voyage, the treasure is ours to collect. If we don't..." He trailed off, his eyes dark with the knowledge of the risks they were taking. "Then our kin will have to be the ones to follow the path we leave behind."

The sea outside whispered its secrets against the hull—once a comforting sound, it now seemed to carry an ominous tone. It was as though the ocean itself had heard their plan and turned cold. Edmund couldn't shake the feeling that they weren't just tampering with treasure—but with fate itself. The chest gleamed between them—a promise of freedom, or damnation. Was this really the best way to ensure their legacy? He shook off the thought. Too late for second-guessing now. They had made their choice.

They had been through too much together to let hesitation cloud their judgement now. Edmund trusted Thomas with his life, and the captain had long since come to see his lieutenant as an equal. There was no one else he would entrust with this plan, no one else he would share such a dangerous secret with.

"Portsmouth." Edmund leaned back in his chair, his gaze distant as his thoughts drifted to their home. "The city's old defences. The towers, the fort… they've stood for centuries. They'll still be there, long after we're gone."

Thomas nodded, a small smile tugging at the corner of his mouth. "We'll leave our marks there, signs only our kin can follow."

Edmund turned his gaze to the chest, the enormity of their decision weighing heavily on him. The Crown would claim the largest portion of the treasure, but the thought of it being lost to time or falling into the wrong hands was unbearable.

"When the treasure is hidden, we write the letters. No sooner." Edmund's voice was firm.

Thomas clapped his hand on his friend's shoulder, his touch as familiar and comforting as a brother's. "We'll make sure it's done right. They'll need both of our letters to find it."

The chest between them glinted in the lantern light. It was a reminder of everything they had fought for—and everything they could lose.

"Just think." Thomas stood and moved to the cabin's small window, his gaze fixed on the dark expanse of sea beyond. "If we survive this, we'll never have to worry again."

Edmund stood beside him, following his gaze out into the inky blackness. "And if we don't?"

Thomas turned, his eyes meeting Edmund's with the same unwavering certainty that had carried them both through years of battle. That confidence, the calm assurance, had always been Thomas' strength. Yet, as Edmund looked into his captain's eyes now, he couldn't help but wonder: was this Thomas' finest trait, or his greatest flaw?

"Then they'll have to be as clever as us. Our blood will know where to begin, but they'll need both letters, and all the wits they've got, to finish the task."

For a moment, the only sound was the soft lap of water against the ship's hull, the world outside the cabin seeming far away.

"We seal the letters in Portsmouth." Edmund broke the silence, his tone steady. "Only once the treasure is safely hidden."

Thomas smiled, the kind of smile reserved for men who had cheated death and lived to tell the tale. "First light, then. We sail for home."

Edmund nodded, though a pit had formed in his stomach. Something about Thomas' confidence, the magnitude of their plan—it all felt so precarious, as if the smallest misstep could send them spiralling into oblivion.

The plan was set, and the bond between them was as strong as it had ever been. Yet beneath the trust and shared purpose, Edmund couldn't shake the feeling of something greater at play—a sense that the steps they took tonight would reverberate not only through their families but through history itself. Whatever the coming days held, they knew they were bound by more than duty—by trust, by friendship, and by the shared understanding that their actions now would resonate through generations to come.

Chapter 10

The cosy warmth of the pub on Spice Island was a welcome contrast to the biting wind that swept through the narrow streets outside. Daniel and Sophie sat at a small table in the corner, their drinks untouched, and the familiar hum of conversation around them providing a comforting backdrop.

Sophie traced the rim of her glass with her finger, lost in thought. "Who do you think she is?" she asked, her voice barely audible over the low murmur of the pub.

Daniel shook his head, leaning back in his chair. "I wish I knew," he replied. "But whoever she is, she's definitely not here by coincidence. She's after something."

A strange feeling of being watched settled over Sophie, but she couldn't place it. It wasn't just the woman they had seen at The Round Tower. Something deeper nagged at her—like they were being drawn into something far bigger than a mere treasure hunt.

Sophie sighed, staring into the flickering flames of the nearby fireplace. "She didn't seem surprised to see us at The Round Tower." Her voice was thoughtful. "Almost like she was expecting us."

"Maybe," Daniel nodded slowly. "But there's no way she could have known we'd be there. We've been following

Edmund's letter, and that's something only we have." He paused, his expression softening. "Honestly, I'm still surprised we've made it this far."

Sophie glanced at him, her interest sparked. "What do you mean?"

Daniel chuckled softly, rubbing the back of his neck. "When we started this whole thing, I didn't really expect to find anything," he admitted. "I thought it would just be a nice adventure—something to do together, a chance to spend some time away from the everyday. A bit of history, a bit of mystery. I wasn't prepared for any of this to be real."

Sophie raised an eyebrow, a smile tugging at the corner of her mouth. "You didn't think we'd find anything?"

"Not really," Daniel confessed, his smile widening. "I mean, sure, I hoped we would, but I wasn't holding my breath. Portsmouth is full of old stories, and I figured this was just another one of those family legends that had grown legs over the years."

Sophie leaned back, her arms crossed, but her expression had softened. "So now that we've actually found something…?"

Daniel shrugged, glancing at the folded letter between them on the table. "Now I'm beginning to think there's more to this than I gave it credit for. We've already uncovered clues, and I have a feeling we're just scratching the surface."

Sophie looked at him, a hint of amusement in her eyes. "So, this wasn't just about the treasure, was it?"

Daniel smiled, his eyes warm. "No, not really. It was about spending time with you, getting lost in a bit of history together."

Despite the warmth in his words, Sophie couldn't shake the unease creeping into her thoughts. There was something else at play here—something they weren't seeing. She leaned forward slightly, lowering her voice. "Do you ever get the feeling we're not the only ones looking?"

Daniel leaned back in his chair, a glint of mischief in his eyes as he sensed the need to lighten the mood. "You know, Spice Island has its own bit of history," he began, his tone shifting. "This whole area was a notorious haunt for smugglers back in the day. The old docks used to be packed with ships from all over the world, and the sailors would come here to unload their cargo—both legal and illegal."

Sophie raised an eyebrow, intrigued. "Illegal cargo? Like what?"

"Rum, tobacco, spices," Daniel explained. "The Crown placed heavy taxes on a lot of goods, so smugglers would bring them in under the radar, slipping them past customs officials. This pub was one of the places they'd meet to do their business."

Sophie glanced around the pub, suddenly seeing it in a different light. "So, this place was a hotspot for criminals?"

Daniel chuckled. "Not quite criminals, but close enough. The whole area was full of shady deals and under-the-table transactions. It wasn't just sailors and merchants either—there were pirates here too, back in the 18th century."

"Pirates?" Sophie's eyes widened. "Seriously?"

"Seriously," Daniel nodded. "This part of Portsmouth has seen it all—smugglers, pirates, soldiers. It's got a long history of being a place where deals are made and fortunes are lost."

Sophie shifted in her seat, the unease returning. If so many secrets had passed through this place, what else was lurking here? What kind of deal were they unknowingly part of now?

"You know," Daniel added with a grin, "there's even a rumour that Lord Nelson had a drink here before heading off to Trafalgar."

Sophie raised an eyebrow, amused. "Lord Nelson, really?"

Daniel was about to continue when the door to the pub creaked open, letting in a sharp gust of cold air. Both he and Sophie turned instinctively toward the entrance.

There she was.

The woman from The Round Tower stepped inside, her eyes scanning the room. She was still dressed in the same mud-caked waders they had seen earlier, her coat buttoned tightly against the chill, and her hair tied back into a loose ponytail. She moved with purpose, her sharp gaze quickly locking onto their table.

Sophie tensed, her heart beating faster.

"Looks like she found us," Daniel muttered under his breath.

The woman approached their table with calm confidence, offering a slight smile as she pulled out a chair. "Mind if I join you?" she asked, her tone casual but with a trace of something unspoken.

Daniel gestured toward the empty chair. "Not at all," he said, his voice neutral but guarded.

The woman settled into the chair, one leg crossed slightly forward as her gaze swept over the table. Her eyes lingered briefly on the letter before returning to Daniel. A faint smile tugged at her lips. "Spice Island," she remarked. "Interesting choice. Full of history, isn't it?"

"Plenty," Daniel replied, his gaze steady. "But I suspect you're more interested in the future than the past."

She tilted her head slightly, her smile widening. "Maybe. But the past always has a way of influencing the future, don't you think?"

Sophie's fingers tensed around her glass. There was something in the woman's voice—something deliberate, as though every word was a piece in a larger game.

The woman's smile faded slightly, her tone becoming more direct. "We're after the same thing, aren't we?"

Daniel raised an eyebrow. "I'm not sure I follow."

She leaned forward slightly, her voice lowering. "The treasure."

Daniel held the woman's gaze, trying to keep his expression neutral. The word "treasure" lingered in the air between them, unspoken but undeniable. Sophie shifted in her seat, her eyes narrowing slightly. A flicker of doubt flashed through her mind—this woman knew too much, and yet, not enough.

"What makes you think we're looking for the same thing?" she asked carefully, her voice steady.

The woman smiled faintly, but there was a sharpness to it. "Let's not play games," she said, her tone measured. "We both know there's more to this than just family history. You've been following clues—so have I. And now we've crossed paths."

Daniel felt his pulse quicken. This woman knew something, but was she baiting them or genuinely following the same trail?

His instincts told him to tread carefully, though his curiosity tugged him forward.

"I'll admit," Daniel began slowly, his tone measured, "we've found a few things. But what exactly is it that you're after?"

The woman's expression shifted, her features growing sharper as her smile disappeared. "The same thing you are," she replied, her voice dropping. "The treasure that's been hidden for centuries. It's out there, waiting to be found. And I think we're closer than either of us realises."

Sophie crossed her arms, her scepticism clear. "And you just happened to show up at The Round Tower while we were there?"

"I've been following my own clues," the woman replied. "The Tower was part of that. I didn't expect to see anyone else there, but I suppose I shouldn't be surprised. This mystery has a way of pulling people in, doesn't it?"

Sophie's eyes flicked to Daniel—was she trying to manipulate them? The woman was too composed, too prepared for this conversation.

Daniel nodded slowly, considering her words. "So, what brought you to Spice Island? Just another clue in your hunt?"

The woman's eyes flicked to the letter on the table. "You could say that. I've been tracing these clues for a while now, and I knew you'd end up here eventually. Spice Island is an important part of Portsmouth's history—just like The Round Tower, just like everything else connected to this."

The way she spoke about history irked Daniel. She wasn't like him—she didn't seem to care about the story behind the treasure, only its value.

Daniel raised an eyebrow. "But why should we trust you? We don't even know your name."

The woman paused, her hesitation barely noticeable before she spoke. "You can call me Claire." Her tone softened slightly, her gaze steady. "I'm not here to take anything from you. We're all chasing the same goal. If we work together, we might actually stand a chance of finding it."

Before Daniel could respond, Claire added smoothly, "And Daniel, Sophie, I already know you're the ones to talk to. Your father was a good man, Daniel."

Both Daniel and Sophie stiffened, exchanging a brief glance. How did she know about their father? The unease that had been bubbling under the surface spiked.

"How do you know who we are?" Daniel asked, his voice carefully controlled.

Claire gave a small, sympathetic smile. "Your father and I crossed paths a few times over the years. He spoke highly of you. That's how I know you're the right ones to work with."

The mention of his father caught Daniel off guard. Was she lying? Or did she really know him? The unease was still there, but something in Claire's tone made it difficult to dismiss her outright. Sophie, too, seemed to relax slightly, though her guard was still up.

Daniel sighed, rubbing his temples. "Look, we've had a long day. We've found some clues, but we're not exactly in a rush to share everything we know."

Claire nodded, her expression softening again. "That's understandable. I didn't come here to force your hand. But maybe we can continue this conversation tomorrow—once we've all had a chance to rest."

Sophie glanced at Daniel, who gave a slight nod. The exhaustion was creeping in, and Claire's calmness, though unnerving, made her seem less of an immediate threat.

"Where are you staying?" Daniel asked, his tone cautious.

"Esk Vale Guest House in Southsea," Claire replied. "It's quiet, a good place to think. If you're up for it, we can all stay there tonight. We'll have plenty of time to compare notes in the morning."

Sophie frowned, but after a moment, she sighed. "It wouldn't hurt to sleep on it," she admitted, glancing at her father.

Daniel agreed, though his wariness hadn't fully faded. "Alright," He gave a brief nod. "We'll stay at Esk Vale tonight, and we can continue this discussion tomorrow."

Claire smiled, but it was brief, as if she knew this was only the beginning of their collaboration. "Great." She rose to her feet. "I'll see you there."

As Claire stood to leave, she paused for a moment, meeting Daniel's gaze. "I meant what I said earlier," her voice soft and sincere. "I'm truly sorry about your father. He seemed like a remarkable man." Daniel blinked, taken aback by her sudden show of sympathy. For a moment, he didn't know how to respond. "Thank you," he managed, his voice quiet.

The vulnerability in his voice startled him. He hadn't expected to feel anything beyond suspicion towards her.

Claire nodded once before turning and walking out of the pub, the door closing softly behind her.

Sophie glanced at Daniel, sensing his discomfort. "That was… unexpected," she murmured.

Daniel's gaze remained fixed on the door. "Yeah," he said, his voice distant. "It was."

They sat in silence for a moment, both processing the strange encounter.

"You think she's genuine?" Sophie asked, breaking the quiet.

Daniel shook his head. "Hard to say. But we're not sharing any more than we have to."

Sophie nodded, then pulled out her phone, tapping the screen a few times.

"What are you doing?" Daniel asked, raising an eyebrow.

Sophie smirked, holding up her phone. "I just booked us a room at Esk Vale Guest House."

Daniel stared at her, eyes wide in surprise. "That quickly?"

Sophie smirked. "It's 2025, Dad. You've got to keep up."

Chapter 11

26th September 1708 – Atlantic Ocean.

The sails strained against the wind as the ship cut through the waves, heading toward England. The vast expanse of the Atlantic stretched before them, but Captain Thomas Hastings knew that their real challenge lay ahead, not at sea, but upon their return to Portsmouth. Beside him, Lieutenant Edmund Grey leaned against the railing, his gaze distant as the two men stood in silence, listening to the creak of the ship and the low hum of the crew at work.

Thomas broke the quiet first. "Do you ever have second thoughts?" he asked quietly, his voice barely audible above the wind.

Edmund turned to look at him, raising an eyebrow. "About what?"

"About this plan." Thomas glanced over his shoulder, ensuring no one was near enough to overhear. "Hiding the treasure, the letters... everything."

Edmund's expression remained calm, but his voice lowered as he replied, "No, I don't. We've come too far to turn back now."

Thomas sighed, his gaze falling on the busy deck below, where the crew bustled about their tasks, oblivious to the secret that he and Edmund carried. "What if something goes wrong? The crew doesn't know what we're planning, but they'll be suspicious if we start moving the treasure."

Edmund shook his head, his voice quiet but steady. "They won't suspect a thing. We'll use only a few trusted hands, and they won't ask questions. They've been told it's part of the captain's orders to move some of the cargo before we dock. Nothing unusual about that."

Thomas nodded, though the worry still lingered in his eyes. "We're cutting it close. If word gets out before we can hide it—"

Edmund interrupted him gently. "It won't. We'll move the treasure before we reach the harbour, under the cover of night. By the time anyone notices it's missing, we'll be long gone."

The two men fell into a comfortable silence again, their bond evident in the ease with which they communicated. Away from the crew, they used first names, a testament to the trust and camaraderie forged through years of war. But as soon as one of the sailors approached to report the condition of the ship, Edmund straightened, his tone shifting.

"Lieutenant Grey." Thomas's tone shifted instantly to formality as a sailor came within earshot. "See to it that the men remain ready for when we make port."

"Aye, Captain," Edmund replied, his voice firm and professional, the mask of naval discipline slipping effortlessly back into place. He exchanged a brief glance with Thomas as the sailor saluted and walked away. They both knew the importance of maintaining the warship's formality. Appearances mattered, especially on a ship where trust and order were vital.

As the sailor disappeared below deck, Edmund resumed his more relaxed posture, turning back to Thomas. "We need to finish this, Thomas. Once we move the treasure, we'll have the rest of the journey to finalise our plans. It's not just for us—it's for our families."

Thomas nodded, though the doubt in his eyes hadn't completely faded. "I know. But it feels... different now. With every mile we get closer to England, I feel the burden of it pressing down on me."

Edmund smiled faintly, a reassuring gesture. "That's because you've always cared too much about doing what's right. But sometimes, what's right for the Crown isn't what's right for us."

Thomas's shoulders relaxed slightly. "I'm just not sure I have your confidence, Edmund."

"You do." Edmund's gaze locked on him, his tone unwavering. "You've been with me every step of the way. I wouldn't have made it this far without you, and I trust you to see this through."

Thomas didn't answer right away. Instead, he gripped the railing, his knuckles white against the salt-stained wood. The ocean stretched endlessly before them, dark and unforgiving, just like the path they had chosen. Though the chest lay hidden below deck, its presence seemed to press on his mind, heavier with each passing mile. Gold coins, jewels—wealth beyond imagining—but the thought of it now felt like an anchor, pulling them deeper into dangerous waters.

"If we're found out, if this goes wrong..." His voice trailed off, a shiver running through him that had nothing to do with the cold. He glanced at Edmund, his eyes dark with the intensity of their decision.

The unspoken understanding passed between them. Despite the formality of their roles, there was a deep bond between them—more than just captain and lieutenant. War had made them brothers, and now, the decision to take the treasure had bound them even closer.

Chapter 12

The cab pulled to a stop in the small car park, which doubled as a driveway for Esk Vale Guest House. The soft glow of the streetlights shimmered on the wet pavement as Sophie stepped out, taking in the cream-painted Victorian house. Flowers hung from baskets by the door, gently swaying in the breeze, adding a quaint charm to the modest building. Yet beneath the surface, the tension of the day lingered—each step toward the guest house heavy with the significance of what they had uncovered.

As they approached the entrance, the door swung open, and Andy, the owner, greeted them with a warm smile. "Evening," he said. "You must be Sophie."

Sophie returned the smile, nodding. "That's right—Sophie Grey."

Andy glanced at his phone, where her booking had already been confirmed. "All sorted then, Miss Grey. Your booking came through perfectly." He handed her the keys with ease. "You're in rooms 4 and 5, just upstairs to the right."

The reception area was small but inviting, with tall ceilings and magnolia walls. The Victorian features, particularly the intricate coving, added a touch of character to the fresh, simple decor. The air inside was heavy with the smell of wood polish, a faint comfort that did little to settle the unease still coiling inside Daniel.

"Breakfast is served from 7:30 a.m.," Andy continued, "and you're welcome to use the dining room this evening if you'd like to relax or bring something to eat. If you need anything, don't hesitate to ask."

"Thanks," Sophie replied, slipping the keys into her pocket and exchanging a glance with Daniel. She could sense her father's mind was elsewhere—preoccupied with the day's discoveries, or perhaps, with Claire.

Andy gave them one last smile before retreating to a private section of the house, leaving them to settle in.

They made their way up the carpeted staircase, each step muffled underfoot. The hallway opened onto a spacious landing before their rooms, its simplicity matching the understated charm of the guest house. There were no windows on the landing, but the tall ceilings and clean walls made the space feel open and inviting.

Sophie unlocked the door to her room, with Daniel following her inside for a brief chat. The room, like the rest of the house, was clean and welcoming. Large windows overlooked the neighbours' gardens, adding a touch of greenery to the peaceful setting. The quiet hum of the suburban night seemed to contrast with the whirlpool of thoughts racing through their minds.

Sophie dropped her phone onto the bed, kicking off her shoes with a sigh of relief.

"I've got to admit." Daniel leaned against the doorframe, his arms crossed loosely. "That check-in was quicker than I expected." His tone carried a hint of distraction, the casual words at odds with the tension in his posture.

Sophie gave him a playful look. "It's 2025, Dad. You've got to keep up."

Daniel chuckled softly, though his thoughts lingered on the day's discoveries. "I didn't think we'd get this far. I figured we'd be home by now—maybe a little wiser, but not with any solid leads."

Sophie settled on the edge of the bed, her expression softening. "It feels like we're really onto something. Today was a good day."

"I wonder if she's already checked in," Sophie mused, looking up at her father. "Claire, I mean."

Daniel crossed the room and settled into the small chair by the window, shifting uncomfortably as he adjusted to the lack of armrests. "Most likely." His voice was thoughtful. "She seems… methodical. I'd be surprised if she didn't plan things out as carefully as we do."

Sophie nodded, tapping her phone absentmindedly before setting it aside. "I still can't quite figure her out. She knew exactly where to find us at the Round Tower. Do you think she's been tracking us?"

Daniel's jaw tightened, the thought gnawing at him since their encounter with Claire. "Tracking us?" He hesitated, his tone cautious. "It's possible. But it might just be coincidence—following the same trail. The Round Tower was an obvious spot for anyone piecing together the clues."

They fell silent for a moment, both reflecting on the day's events. The discovery at the Round Tower had been more significant than either of them expected, and the cryptic carving of the 'G' had lingered in Daniel's mind ever since.

"I still can't stop thinking about that inscription." Sophie broke the silence, her fingers lightly tapping the edge of the bed. "We've already figured out it's pointing us to Southsea Castle, but I keep wondering... why there? What's the connection to Edmund?"

Daniel leaned back as far as the chair allowed, his gaze thoughtful as he processed her words. "It makes sense historically—Southsea Castle was Henry VIII's fortress, built to defend Portsmouth. Maybe that's the link: a place of power, and something personal to Edmund's father, tied to the king's watch."

Sophie nodded slowly, her thoughts churning. "It feels like there's always more to this. It's not just about where the king stood. There's got to be another layer, another clue we're missing."

Daniel smiled faintly, impressed by her intuition. "You're right. There's still more ahead, and Southsea Castle is only part of it. Whatever's waiting for us there might point to the next piece of the puzzle."

Sophie sighed, leaning back on the bed. "It feels like we're getting somewhere, but there's still so much we don't know."

"We're not far off," Daniel replied, his voice calm. "But we need to be careful with Claire. She's holding back, I can feel it. We can't show all our cards just yet."

Sophie nodded in agreement. "Yeah, I got that impression too. She's playing it close to the chest, and I don't think we can trust her fully—at least not yet."

Daniel rubbed his temples, his mind racing. "Tomorrow, when we meet her, we'll compare notes. But we'll only give her what we're comfortable sharing. I want to see what she knows before we reveal too much."

Sophie smirked. "You're thinking like a pirate."

Daniel chuckled softly. "Maybe I am. But we've come too far to lose the upper hand now."

Sophie stood up, stretching slightly as she moved to the window. "Do you think the clues will take us straight to the treasure?"

"I doubt it," Daniel's voice heavy with thought. "I think there's still more to uncover—more pieces of the puzzle. Southsea Castle might be the next step, but I have a feeling it won't be the final destination."

Sophie turned back to face him. "So, tomorrow we meet Claire. Compare notes. But we keep the most important parts to ourselves. Agreed?"

"Agreed," Daniel replied, standing up as well. "And let's not forget—she's probably thinking the same thing. We'll have to tread carefully."

Chapter 13

The headlights of Claire's car cut through the misty night as she drove along the quiet road toward Eastney Beach. The rain had eased to a light drizzle, casting a sheen on the road, reflecting the soft glow of the streetlights. She cracked the window slightly, allowing the briny scent of the sea air to mingle with the faint odour of rain-soaked earth. The briny air was a sharp reminder of the years she had spent chasing this treasure—years of sacrifice, of false leads, and dwindling hope. But not tonight. Tonight, something had shifted.

Finding Daniel and Sophie Grey earlier today had not been a stroke of luck. It had been part of a carefully executed plan. Just hours ago, the private investigator had sent her the message that changed everything. She could still see the words illuminated on her phone screen: "They're active. Daniel Grey and his daughter are in Portsmouth." Her heart had skipped a beat when she read it. After all these years of chasing shadows, this was the closest she'd ever come to the treasure. The private investigator, the same man who had kept a watchful eye from the shadows, had been worth every penny. He had been watching Daniel and Sophie for weeks, providing her with just enough insight to stay one step ahead.

For months, she had been knee-deep in the mud at Fareham Creek, scouring the marshlands, her drone buzzing above the murky waters, capturing nothing but disappointment. Every search felt like a step further from her goal, the clues in her ancestor's letter leading her in circles. It had become an obsession—a frustrating, all-consuming pursuit. The mud clung to her boots as she packed up her drone, her mind already racing ahead to Portsmouth, to the next move.

Now, as she pulled up along the promenade at Eastney Beach, Claire's mind wandered back to that moment—the realisation that Daniel had inherited the letter from his father. It hadn't been easy with him. She had tried to gain access to the letter many times over the years, always approaching with the same calm professionalism, yet always leaving empty-handed. Daniel's father had been cautious, too cautious. He had dismissed her every request, never once considering that the contents of that letter might unlock something far bigger than an old family story.

He had believed the letter to be just an heirloom, something best left in the past. Even when Claire had hinted at treasure, he'd remained resolute. Treasure or not, he had said, nothing good could come from digging up the past.

Claire's hands clenched around the steering wheel, the memory still vivid. She had respected him—more than she cared to acknowledge. His caution was frustrating, but in a way, she had admired it. He wasn't blinded by greed or ambition. He had simply seen the letter as a relic of history, not a map to fortune. That had made it all the more difficult to accept that the only way she'd had the opportunity to see the letter was through his death.

A part of her felt conflicted. It wasn't her way to wish harm upon people, and yet here she was, benefiting from a loss she hadn't planned for. She had to push down that guilt—there was no room for it now. Daniel had inherited the letter, and the game had changed. It wasn't just about following a trail anymore; it was about catching up.

She had been tracking Daniel for weeks. The private investigator had been her eyes, ensuring that when Daniel finally decided to act on the family secret, she'd be there. She hadn't intended to cross paths with them today, but when she heard about The Round Tower, she knew it was time to confront them. The private investigator had done his job well.

Now, as she parked her car along the promenade, the sea stretching out in front of her, Claire sat back in her seat, the sound of waves steady against the shore. The shoreline was empty, the quiet only broken by the rhythmic crash of the waves against the pebbles. She had grown used to these moments—sitting in her car, staring out at the water, letting the isolation of the sea calm her restless mind. But tonight, the waves didn't calm her. They echoed her determination, her need to see this through.

There was more at stake now than there ever had been before. Daniel and Sophie had found something, she was sure of it. Their clues were connected—pieces of a puzzle that had eluded her for too long. She clenched the steering wheel, her knuckles whitening. For years, she had believed that her ancestor's letter was the key to it all, but now... now she knew that Daniel's letter held the missing piece. It had to.

Leaning her head against the car seat, she stared out at the dark sea. She had been chasing the treasure for so long, she sometimes wondered if she had lost sight of why. The thrill of discovery? The promise of wealth? Or was it something deeper, something far more personal? The legacy of her family weighed heavily on her shoulders, and every failure felt like a betrayal to her ancestors.

Her obsession had cost her more than she cared to admit—relationships had withered, friendships faded. The chase had devoured her, leaving little room for anything else. What would she be, if not the one to find the treasure?

She reached over to the passenger seat, where her drone rested. She had scouted Fareham Creek earlier today, following her ancestor's vague directions, but it had yielded little. The images on the drone's monitor replayed in her mind—marshes, thick reeds, the endless stretch of grey mud. It was all wrong. She had been looking in the wrong places, led astray by the puzzle pieces that refused to fit. But something Daniel said tonight had changed everything. The clues they had uncovered at The Round Tower were precise. They pointed to something far more tangible than her ancestor's cryptic directions ever had. She needed to know what was in his letter.

Tomorrow, she'd find out.

Sitting up, Claire glanced at the rear-view mirror, catching her own reflection. Her hair was still slightly damp from earlier, the tendrils curling from the mist in the air. She had changed into dry clothes after leaving Spice Island, but her mind was still racing, even as her body began to tire.

Turning the key in the ignition, Claire didn't start the engine right away. She let her gaze drift over the dark expanse of the sea, a growing sense of anticipation ate at her. Tomorrow, they would need to compare notes. But she wouldn't reveal too much. Not yet. Her fingers tapped rhythmically on the steering wheel as she planned her next move. She needed to play this carefully—extract as much information as possible from Daniel and Sophie without tipping her hand. They were close, closer than they realised, but she wasn't about to lose everything by trusting them too quickly.

After a few moments, Claire started the car and pulled away from the promenade, the headlights casting long beams across the wet road. The route to Esk Vale Guest House was a straight drive along the coast, the sea on one side, the quiet streets of Southsea on the other. She kept her window cracked open slightly, the fresh tang of the sea breeze helping to clear her thoughts.

Her patience had been rewarded today, but she knew it wouldn't last forever. Tomorrow, things would have to move faster. Daniel held the key to everything, and she couldn't afford to wait much longer.

Chapter 14

The breakfast room at Esk Vale Guest House had a simple charm, blending its Victorian elegance with a cosy, lived-in feel. The pastel yellow and green walls brightened the space, while the tall ceiling featured a 1930s-style chandelier that added a subtle touch of grandeur. A white marble fireplace, though unlit, drew the eye, with its mantel neatly arranged with orchids, their soft blooms providing a fresh contrast to the room's period details. The Victorian covings framed the room with a nod to its history. Despite the warmth of the setting, there was a tension in the air that even the inviting decor couldn't ease. Oak tables and comfortable chairs were scattered about, encouraging guests to linger over breakfast—though none seemed in a hurry to do so.

Daniel and Sophie's table was no exception. The remnants of their full English breakfast lay pushed aside, untouched for the better part of the morning. Daniel stirred his tea absentmindedly, glancing occasionally toward the door, his mind far from the cosy setting. Sophie, usually energetic and chatty, tapped lightly on her phone, distracted. The room felt like a calm before a storm, with each passing second pulling them further into the unknown.

"I wonder if she's even staying here," Sophie remarked, her eyes drifting to the clock on the wall. The end of breakfast service loomed, the minutes ticking away with increasing impatience. Claire had yet to show.

Daniel shrugged slightly, though there was a hint of doubt in his expression. "She'll show," he muttered, more to convince himself than Sophie. But even as he said it, a faint doubt settled over him, clinging at the edges of his thoughts. Was this all a mistake?

As if on cue, the door to the breakfast room opened, and Claire stepped in. The soft creak of the door sent a jolt through the quiet room, and Daniel felt his pulse quicken, though he kept his expression neutral. Gone was the rugged, mud-spattered figure from their previous encounter. Claire had freshened up—her hair now sleek and neatly styled, her complexion glowing as though she had washed away the strain of the day before. She wore a simple, fitted top paired with jeans, exuding a relaxed yet effortlessly attractive air.

In the soft morning light streaming through the windows, she looked striking—almost disarming. Yet, beneath her composed demeanour, Daniel sensed something else—an unspoken urgency, masked by her steady walk. She moved toward them with a purposeful stride, her eyes scanning the room before landing on Daniel and Sophie.

There was something about her transformation that gave Sophie pause. The woman who stood before them now appeared more confident, more polished—dangerously so. In that moment, the quiet room seemed to shrink, the space between them brimming with the tension of what was about to unfold.

Andy, the polite and attentive owner of the guest house, approached with his notepad in hand, a welcoming smile on his face. "Good morning," he greeted, glancing between them. "Just in time for breakfast. What can I get you?"

"Morning, Andy," Claire responded with a polite smile. "Just toast and a coffee, please."

Andy scribbled the order down and made his usual small talk. "Looks like the weather might improve later this morning, though it's a bit windy out there right now."

Claire nodded in acknowledgment. "Hopefully it clears up soon," she replied, though her tone seemed detached, her mind clearly elsewhere.

"Well, if you need anything else, just give me a shout." Andy offered a friendly grin before heading back toward the kitchen.

As soon as Andy disappeared, the atmosphere shifted. The gentle murmur of the TV seemed to fade into the background, replaced by a tangible tension that gripped the room. Daniel exchanged a quick look with Sophie, both of them aware that this meeting could change everything.

Claire took her seat with careful precision, her eyes shifting between Daniel and Sophie. She knew what they had uncovered, and her presence hinted at something far more serious than a simple breakfast conversation. For a moment, they sat in silence, the atmosphere tense and expectant. The quiet between them had shifted, no longer easy but stretched thin, as if something pivotal hung just beyond reach.

Sophie tapped the table softly, her fingers betraying her nerves. Claire's calm exterior felt almost unnerving, as though she was always two steps ahead, already knowing what cards they held. The letter, folded carefully inside Daniel's coat pocket, felt like a heavy secret, its edges brushing against his chest, reminding him that soon, they would have to lay it on the table—perhaps literally.

"So," Claire began, breaking the silence. Her voice was calm but carried a weight that demanded attention. "We've all come too far to keep circling around this. Let's figure out how much we're each willing to share."

Daniel and Sophie exchanged a glance. This was the moment they had anticipated, but it still felt like standing on the edge of an unknown abyss. The letter in Daniel's pocket seemed heavier than ever, a reminder of what was at stake.

"Agreed." Daniel's tone was measured, though tension crept into his posture. Slowly, he reached for the letter, aware that this decision could shift everything between them. Keeping it hidden wasn't an option anymore.

The air in the breakfast room felt heavier now, a quiet tension settling between the three of them. Claire's toast and coffee sat untouched as her sharp eyes moved between the two of them. Sophie adjusted in her chair, her movements subtle but protective. Daniel held Claire's gaze, his expression carefully neutral as he weighed his next words.

"We've followed some clues," Daniel began cautiously, "but let's be clear—we're not about to share everything."

Claire took a slow sip of her coffee, unfazed. "Of course, I wouldn't expect you to. But if we're chasing the same goal, maybe it's time we see where our paths converge."

Daniel laid the worn letter on the table, tapping the faded parchment lightly. "This letter was written by my ancestor, Lieutenant Edmund Grey, before his last voyage. It tells of the treasure they captured on the Spanish galleon, La Fortuna, and how they brought it back to England. So far, it has guided us through Portsmouth, from The Round Tower to Southsea Castle."

Claire's eyes flicked to the letter, her expression betraying a flicker of recognition. "So, Southsea Castle," Claire repeated, her tone thoughtful. "That's where you think the next clue leads?"

Daniel gave a small nod, cautious as ever. "The letter talks about 'where the watchtower meets the sea,' and we found a marking beneath the tower in weathered stone. That leads to Southsea Castle—where 'the king stood watch.'"

Sophie, who had been mostly observing, chimed in, "Well, we think it points to Southsea Castle. The king—it could be referencing Henry VIII, right?" She paused, her gaze narrowing slightly. "How do you seem to know so much about this? Have you been following similar clues?"

Claire smiled faintly, her eyes steady on Sophie. "I've done my research, yes. But Edmund Grey wasn't the only one involved in this. Thomas Hastings—my ancestor—served with him. They fought together when they took La Fortuna in the Caribbean. They were on the same ship when they captured the treasure."

Both Daniel and Sophie leaned forward slightly, their interest heightened.

"The ship they sailed on was HMS Endeavour. ," Claire continued, her voice steady. "It was their mission in the Caribbean that led them to La Fortuna, filled with riches beyond expectation. But when they returned to England, not everything went to the Crown."

Daniel's eyes widened slightly, his curiosity obvious. "Not everything?"

Claire nodded. "That's where the letters come in. Edmund Grey and Thomas Hastings separated part of the treasure before reaching England. They left clues for their families, clues they hoped would lead their descendants to the hidden gold if they never made it back."

Sophie exchanged a quick glance with her father, a mixture of disbelief and excitement in her expression. "So they hid some of the treasure?"

Claire leaned back slightly, her eyes never leaving Daniel's. "That's my theory. Both Edmund and Thomas left letters, each with their own set of clues. Together, these letters can lead us to what they hid before the rest was handed over to the Crown."

Daniel tapped the edge of Edmund's letter, deep in thought. "And you've followed Thomas' letter?"

Claire nodded, pulling out her ancestor's letter and placing it beside Daniel's. "Thomas wrote this before their final voyage. It speaks of 'where the old stones stand watch,' just like Edmund's letter. Together, I believe these clues will reveal the full path."

Sophie studied the two letters carefully. "Why now?" she asked, her voice quiet but firm. "Why are you just showing up now?"

Claire met her gaze. "Because until recently, I didn't have enough to go on. I've been tracing my family's history for years, following the fragments of Thomas' clues. But it wasn't until I learned that Edmund Grey's family had a similar letter that it all started to make sense. You're the key to this. Together, I believe we can solve it."

Daniel remained cautious, but there was no denying the depth of Claire's knowledge. She knew the names, the history, the details that had brought them this far. And yet, despite her transparency, there was still an air of mystery surrounding her motivations.

"So," Claire continued, her voice steady, "I think it's time we stop working separately and start working together. We've both come too far to let the trail slip away now. Let's pool our knowledge and see where it leads us."

The breakfast room remained quiet, with only the low murmur of the TV news in the background. The smell of fresh toast and coffee lingered in the air, but none of them seemed focused on eating. Daniel, Sophie, and Claire sat at the table, the two letters—one from Edmund Grey and the other from Captain Thomas Hastings—spread out in front of them.

Sophie tapped the edge of Claire's letter with her finger. "This first part," she began, scanning the lines, "'where the old stones stand watch, where the sea meets the land.' That's got to be The Round Tower, right?"

Claire shook her head slowly. "No," she replied. "At first, I thought that too. But after going over it carefully, I'm convinced it's pointing towards Southsea Castle instead."

Sophie frowned in confusion. "But we found clues at The Round Tower."

Daniel cleared his throat, the moment settling over him as he picked up the fragile letter. "It all started with Edmund's letter," he began, his voice steady but carrying an undertone of significance. Carefully adjusting the brittle parchment, he glanced at the others to ensure their attention before continuing. With a deliberate pause, he smoothed the aged paper and began to read aloud, his tone respectful, almost reverent:

"Father,

15th August, 1708. We took the Spanish galleon, La Fortuna, in the Caribbean. Her holds brimmed with wealth, more than any of us could have imagined. The journey home has been long and fraught with danger—storms, enemy vessels, the constant threat of betrayal. Many good men were lost, far too many. If you are reading this, Father, it means that the sea has claimed me as well. But what we brought back, that which was fought for and won, still remains. When my path is lost to the sea, look for the light that has guided our family through the storm.

Beneath it lies the memory of the past, written in glass for all to see.

Seek where our family once stood, where the watchtower meets the sea. There you will find the first sign, our mark weathered in stone.

The sixth rose, a bridge too far, guards the secret, an arch scar. Follow where the land meets the tides, where the stones bear the weight of our history.

In my absence, this task falls to you, seek a friend not foe. Only the careful eye will unravel the path. May you and our legacy survive the test of time.

Lieutenant Edmund Grey."

Daniel paused, his fingers gently tracing the edges of the letter. The paper was worn and yellowed, its corners frayed by time. Each stroke of the handwriting had been carefully etched, yet the passage of history seemed to press upon the faded ink. It felt as though the letter had weathered the same storms Edmund Grey had once faced, just as fragile as the secrets it held within.

"We can't afford to misread any of this," Daniel added softly, his brow tense. "Every word here feels like a test—one small mistake, and we might miss what they intended to hide."

Claire leaned in slightly, listening with rapt attention.

Holding up the letter for Claire to see, Daniel pointed to the distinctive 'G' in Edmund's signature. "See this 'G'? It's the same as the one we found carved at The Round Tower," he explained. "That carving led us to the base of the tower, where we uncovered the message: 'To the fortress by the sea, where the king stood watch.' That's when we realized Southsea Castle had to be our next stop."

Sophie chimed in with growing excitement. "We're hoping to find the connection to 'the sixth rose' when we get there."

Claire listened, a flicker of confusion on her face. "But your letter from Edmund doesn't mention a fort or castle directly."

Daniel nodded in agreement. "True. The connection only became clear after we found the carving at The Round Tower. It's like the pieces are slowly falling into place."

Sophie could feel the momentum between them building. The pieces were starting to fall into place. She turned to Claire, her voice steady but direct. "Claire, you've studied this as much as we have. Do you think Thomas' letter could give us any clues about the next step?"

Daniel watched Claire as Sophie spoke, sensing that she held a crucial part of the puzzle. "We've come further than I ever imagined, and your insight could really push us forward."

Claire paused, her gaze distant as she absorbed the moment, then nodded thoughtfully. "When I read Thomas' letter, I realized we weren't just looking for one location." She adjusted her posture slightly. "He wrote..."

'To my son,

There are times in life when one's course, though carefully charted, must take unexpected turns. Events have unfolded that I did not foresee, leading to decisions made out of necessity, rather than choice. We have faced dangers, navigated treacherous waters, and come across fortune beyond expectation, but not without cost. Many men have sacrificed more than gold can ever repay. Be mindful of this burden and tread carefully, for not all roads are meant to be travelled alone. Seek those who can share in this weight—a trustworthy hand will always help to lighten the load.

When my path is lost to the sea, you must look where the old stones stand watch, where the sea meets the land and ancient towers guard the coast. It is there that you will find the first signs.

At the fort, short and stout, where the cannon faced the sea, lies the key, our mark that would have guided you with light.

Ascend to where the wind meets the stone and sky, your feet point where tides flow. Follow the unseen path, where the waters bend.

When the sea turns to land and the tides no longer call, seek where time has swallowed the truth. Follow the waters beyond, where the land surrenders to the pull of the sea. Beyond the bend, where the river meets the earth, a bridge of stone will guide your way.

Captain Thomas Hastings.'

Claire glanced down at her letter, its edges singed from her earlier attempts to reveal hidden writing. She bit her lip, feeling an awkward heat rise in her cheeks. "I, uh... I thought maybe there was a hidden message. Lemon juice. You know, the old spy trick? But nothing showed up, just a few burns."

Daniel exchanged a glance with Sophie. "It seems like our clues have given us a clearer path to follow."

"Which is why," Claire continued, leaning back slightly, "I believe that with both letters, we might be able to fill in the blanks. Thomas' letter mentions, 'At the fort, short and stout, where the cannon faced the sea, lies the key, our mark that would have guided you with light.' The letters were meant to be used together, weren't they? Your path may have led you through Portsmouth, but my clues could unlock the rest."

Sophie looked between the two of them. "It's starting to make sense. Each letter holds part of the story, but together they lead to the whole treasure."

Daniel studied Claire carefully, noticing the frustration behind her words. "So you haven't found any solid path from your letter yet?"

Claire's lips tightened into a thin line. "No. Not yet. But with your progress and these clues, we're closer than we've ever been."

Sophie couldn't shake the growing sense of unease, a creeping doubt that Claire might be right—if they didn't use both letters, they might never find the treasure. Her fingers traced the edges of Edmund's letter, their lifeline to a centuries-old secret.

Daniel nodded, his fingers tapping the edge of the table thoughtfully. "Thomas' letter also mentions 'Follow the unseen path, where the waters bend.' We'll need to keep an open mind when we reach Southsea Castle. Both letters point to key locations, but they might be intertwined in ways we haven't fully understood yet."

Sophie nodded. "It feels like we're piecing together fragments of a map. Let's hope Southsea Castle fills in the missing parts."

The tension in the room softened, though Daniel and Sophie still eyed Claire warily. They were all heading to Southsea Castle now, but they would need to stay cautious, keeping parts of their knowledge to themselves until they were sure they could trust each other fully.

As Claire leaned back, she gave the letters one last glance, the charred edges a stark reminder of her desperation. She knew this might be her final chance to solve the mystery—one wrong move, and it could all go up in flames.

As they stood from the table, Claire glanced back at the letters one last time, her voice calm but determined. "I believe we're close. Together, I think we can figure this out."

Chapter 15

11ᵗʰ October 1708 – Atlantic Ocean.

The dim cabin of *HMS Endeavour.* swayed with the rhythm of the waves as Lieutenant Edmund Grey sat across from Captain Thomas Hastings. Between them, the flickering flame of an oil lamp cast shifting shadows over the map spread on the table. The English coast was now just a few weeks away, and the final phase of their plan weighed heavily on their minds.

Thomas stood by the small porthole, his eyes fixed on the moonlit waters beyond. He turned to Edmund, his expression firm. "It's time we finalize the details. Before we dock in Portsmouth, we need to secure it where no one will find it."

Edmund leaned over the map, his fingers tracing the coastline. "A quiet inlet," he murmured. "Away from the prying eyes of the Crown's officials. The barrels of rum will be our cover."

Thomas nodded. "Rum smuggling isn't unusual. But what's inside those barrels…" He didn't need to finish the sentence. The gold, taken from the Spanish galleon *La Fortuna*, lay hidden in the ship's hold, waiting to be smuggled ashore.

"We'll need trusted hands," Edmund's voice steady under the strain of their secret. "Men who will follow orders without asking too many questions."

Thomas turned, moving to the table, his expression thoughtful. "I've chosen a few—Harper, Briggs, and Ward. They think they're smuggling rum, and that's all they need to know. They'll help us offload the barrels before we reach Portsmouth. Once ashore, we take the treasure straight to the hiding place by boat."

Edmund studied the names. Harper was a seasoned sailor, loyal and sharp. Briggs, quiet and reliable. Ward, eager to prove himself. They were the right choices. Men who wouldn't pry but who could be trusted to do their job.

"The men will never suspect what's inside," Thomas continued, his voice low. "As far as they're concerned, it's rum for sale in some backwater tavern. We offload the barrels at a secluded spot along the coast, then ferry them to the final destination. They won't ask questions if we pay them well enough."

Edmund sat back, nodding. "And the letters? When do we make the marks?"

Thomas's expression hardened, his tone leaving no room for debate. "Not until it's done. Once the treasure is secure, we'll seal the letters. Our closest kin will have the clues, but no one else. Not even the men helping us."

There was a pause, with an unspoken trust hanging between the two men. This was their legacy—treasure hidden from the Crown, not for greed, but for their families, should they not live to reclaim it themselves. A quiet understanding lingered in the pause, carrying the trust they'd placed in each other and their legacy.

Edmund's gaze turned distant, his thoughts drifting to the future. "They'll never know what we've done here," he murmured, his voice barely audible. "No one will. And those who do—"

"—won't live long enough to tell the tale," Thomas finished. There was a coldness in his words, but a resolve too. They had no choice but to see it through. Failure wasn't an option, not with so much at stake.

Thomas leaned over the map, his finger pressing firmly on a stretch of coastline near their intended landing. "We'll unload the barrels here." His voice was steady as he traced the route. "Once ashore, we'll move them straight to the hiding place by boat. It's remote, quiet, and no one will suspect a thing about a few rum barrels."

Edmund frowned slightly. "What if someone stumbles upon the barrels before we retrieve them?"

"They won't," Thomas replied confidently. "We'll move them under the cover of night. The men will think they're just doing a favour for their captain—nothing more."

The cabin lapsed into silence once more, the enormity of their plan sinking in. The treasure they had taken had the power to reshape their futures, but it came with a price—a burden that would linger with them for the rest of their lives.

Edmund stood and stepped toward the side of the cabin, his gaze fixed on the dark expanse of sea beyond. "We're so close now."

Thomas joined him, his gaze steely. "Once the barrels are moved, there's no turning back."

They stood side by side, as they had through countless trials, their bond forged in blood and unwavering trust. This was no different—another challenge, another adversary, only this time the stakes were even higher. Thomas clapped Edmund on the shoulder, a gesture of warmth between two men who had long been comrades.

Thomas's gaze hardened, his voice low and resolute. "We've come this far. We'll see it through."

Edmund nodded, the reality of the plan sinking in. "Aye," he agreed. "We'll see it through."

Chapter 16

The view of Southsea Castle didn't quite match Sophie's expectations. Her eyes narrowed as they neared, taking in the understated outline of the fortress with a touch of surprise.

"Is this Southsea Castle?" she muttered under her breath, the surprise evident in her tone. "It looks... different than I imagined. Where are the turrets? And what's with the lighthouse?" She glanced at Daniel. "I thought castles were meant to dominate the landscape, not... doubling as a lighthouse."

Before Daniel could answer, Claire chimed in with a pointed look. "Sophie, remember Thomas' letter. 'At the fort, short and stout, where the cannon faced the sea...' This is exactly the kind of place we should be looking for. Southsea Castle wasn't built for grandeur—it was built for function." She pulled out her letter and read aloud once more, as if to reaffirm her conviction. "'The key, our mark that would have guided you with light.' It fits, don't you think?"

Sophie glanced at Claire, her scepticism wavering. "I guess, but I still don't see how this place fits with what I expected from a castle."

Daniel stepped in, taking the opportunity to explain. "Southsea Castle was never designed to look like the castles in the stories, Sophie. Henry VIII ordered its construction in 1544, not to inspire awe, but to defend Portsmouth from a potential French invasion. The low profile was intentional. It was easier to defend, harder to target from the sea."

"And the lighthouse?" Sophie prompted, raising an eyebrow.

"That came later," Daniel replied, gesturing toward the tower. "It was added in the early 19th century. But long before the lighthouse, there would have been a beacon—a signal fire used to warn ships and communicate with other defences around the harbour. It would have served a similar purpose as a navigation aid, guiding vessels or signalling danger." He paused, reflecting on the significance. "That's probably what Thomas' letter is referencing—'guided you with light.'" He echoed Claire's reading.

They approached the wooden bridge spanning the castle's moat. Sophie stopped, tilting her head as she studied the rocky trench below. "This doesn't look like a typical moat." Her voice carried a hint of confusion. "It's dry."

Daniel nodded. "It always has been. This moat wasn't filled with water; it was designed as an extra line of defence against ground assaults. Any attackers would have had to climb down and up again before reaching the castle walls."

Sophie seemed to absorb the information, nodding slowly as her eyes drifted over the castle's thick stone walls. "It's more practical than I thought," she admitted. "But it's still strange to think of a castle without any water surrounding it."

As they crossed the bridge, Daniel's gaze shifted upwards to the coat of arms carved into the stone above the gate. His steps faltered for a moment, eyes narrowing in thought. "That coat of arms…" he began, trailing off. "It's from Charles II's reign. I'd almost forgotten about the modifications that were made to the castle during his time."

Claire noticed the shift in Daniel's demeanour. "Does that change anything?" she asked, her eyes narrowing with curiosity.

Daniel scratched his chin, staring at the emblem. "The clue at the Round Tower mentioned a king. I assumed it referred to Henry VIII, but maybe it's pointing to something broader than just him—perhaps to the history of the castle or its defences."

Sophie shrugged, indifferent. "Does it really matter which monarch? Either way, we're still following the clues. The castle's been here for centuries—whatever we're looking for is tied to its history, not just one ruler." Yet, an uneasy feeling clung to her, a quiet sense of being watched that had lingered since their journey began. It was subtle, like a pair of unseen eyes tracking their every step. She glanced back quickly, but the path behind them remained empty.

"It's possible," Daniel admitted, his voice tinged with uncertainty. "But considering when this letter was written, it was Queen Anne who was on the throne. Her reign was important for a lot of reasons, not just politically. The War of Spanish Succession was happening, and the British Navy was crucial to her strategy. If the treasure connects to her time, it may be tied to naval expansion, or maybe even the tensions with Spain, given the period."

They paused at the castle's entrance, the air heavy with unspoken questions. Daniel felt a flicker of doubt, sensing that one wrong move could cost them everything. Yet, deep down, a glimmer of hope remained—perhaps this castle still held the answers they sought. They had reached a point where every assumption could either lead them closer to the treasure or send them spiralling off course.

"Let's get inside." Claire's voice was low, her steps deliberate as she moved toward the entrance. "We need to start from the beginning and look for anything we might have missed."

They entered the courtyard, the wide-open space framed by thick walls. Claire remained focused, scanning every stone. "Thomas' letter mentions a mark. We may find something like an 'H' for Hastings, or perhaps a Tudor rose—something carved into the stone."

Daniel nodded, though his gaze drifted towards the ramparts. "It's possible. Thomas and Edmund would have left their clues near something significant."

They climbed the stone steps up to the ramparts. From there, the view opened up across the Solent, the sea glittering under the pale sky. Cannons, weathered by time but still formidable, lined the ramparts.

Claire walked along the ramparts, her eyes scanning the walls intently. As she stepped closer to one of the cannons, she recited Thomas' letter, her voice steady. "'*Where the cannon faced the sea, lies the key, our mark that would have guided you with light.*'"

She turned to Daniel and Sophie, her expression sharp with focus. "If Thomas left his mark, it would be near these defences—the cannons, the walls—they were central to the castle's purpose. We need to check everything carefully."

They moved along the ramparts, eyes scanning every stone. Claire's gaze sharpened. "We'll find it," she said firmly. "Whatever clue Thomas left, it's here."

As they stood on the ramparts, the cold wind coming in off the Solent, Daniel's expression grew more serious. His gaze shifted from the ancient cannons to the red brickwork that surrounded them.

Claire noticed the change in his demeanour. "What is it?" she asked, sensing the unease in his silence.

Daniel sighed, running his hand along the stone edge of the wall. "If Thomas made any marks around the ramparts, as the clue suggests, there's a good chance they've been lost to the modifications. The cannons, the pivots, the brickwork—they weren't here during Thomas' time. Most of this was rebuilt during the Napoleonic Wars."

Claire tilted her head slightly, her eyes narrowing in confusion. "The Napoleonic Wars? When exactly was that?"

"1803 to 1815," Daniel replied. "During the reign of George III. The castle was heavily fortified during that time. These cannons and the gun pivots were added then, along with the red brick you see along the walls. A lot of what was originally here may have been altered or destroyed."

He gestured towards the crenels along the wall. "And where once stood cannons aimed through those openings, there are now potted olive trees. It's strange, isn't it? Tools of war replaced by symbols of peace. These walls, once built to repel invaders, now shelter something far more serene."

Claire followed his gaze to the pale green leaves swaying gently in the breeze. "Maybe that's a good thing." Her voice was soft, thoughtful. "But I doubt Thomas would have seen it that way."

Her words lingered in the air, and as Daniel considered them, a realisation struck him. Despite their initial resolve not to reveal too much to Claire, here they were, laying their progress bare. Daniel hadn't even noticed it happening until now. Claire's smooth, subtle approach had coaxed more from them than he intended. It was unsettling, yet impressive in its own right. For all his caution, he had to admit—she had a talent for pulling threads of information with effortless finesse.

Claire's face fell slightly as she absorbed his words. "So, you're saying we might be too late? That the clue could be gone?"

Daniel hesitated but gave a small nod. "It's possible." He gestured to the heavy gun pivots. "These pivots are actually recycled cannon barrels. The modifications would have required tearing up the original stone foundations. Any mark Thomas may have left could have been destroyed or covered up during the work."

Sophie frowned, stepping closer to the cannons, her eyes searching the ground for any hint of the past. "But there must be something left. Thomas wouldn't have left us with nothing."

For a moment, the scale of their quest felt overwhelming to Sophie—could centuries of history have truly erased the clues they had been so desperately chasing?

Claire pulled out her letter, her fingers brushing over the familiar parchment. She handed it to Daniel, her voice quieter now. "What do you think? Is there anything in this that could help?"

Daniel took the letter, his eyes scanning the faded script. He read aloud, *"Ascend to where the wind meets the stone and sky, your feet point where tides flow."* He paused, considering the words. "This... this sounds like it could be pointing us to the main tower—the highest point of the castle."

Sophie looked up at the structure rising above them. "The lighthouse?"

"Not exactly," Daniel replied, shaking his head. "The tower itself. We should head up there and check. If Thomas left a clue, it would make sense to put it somewhere with a clear view of the sea—where the wind and tides meet."

They made their way to the top of the tower, climbing the narrow worn steps. Once they reached the top, the wind whipped at their clothes, the chill stronger at this height. From here, they could see the vast stretch of the Solent, the horizon blending into the distant Isle of Wight.

Sophie scanned the stone walls around them, her fingers tracing the rough surface. "If there was a clue up here, it's not obvious."

Daniel frowned, moving closer to one of the gun platforms. "There's no sign of anything," he muttered. "No carvings, no marks... nothing."

Claire stepped beside him, her frustration evident. "Could it have been covered up again?"

Daniel nodded. "It's a real possibility. Just like at the Round Tower, when we searched the top and found that waterproofing material had been added. Any clue that might have been left would have been sealed under layers of modifications."

His gaze shifted to the outer boundary. "And with the recent sea defence restoration, any original markings along the castle's edge would have been buried under the new stonework, further protecting the castle from the sea."

Sophie's gaze dropped as the full meaning of their discovery set in. "So... the clue is gone?

"Not necessarily," Daniel's voice firm but uncertain. "We've already seen how time can change these places, like with the Round Tower. Maybe there's still something here we're overlooking—something Thomas wouldn't have expected to be erased."

Claire looked out over the sea, her eyes narrowing against the wind. "But where does that leave us? If Thomas' clue is covered or gone, how do we move forward?"

Daniel thought for a moment, his eyes flickering with determination. "We keep going. We've come this far, and even if some clues are lost, others remain. There's always something we're missing, and it might not be as obvious as we think."

Sophie glanced out over the sea, her mind racing with the history surrounding them. She spoke, almost to herself. "Even though there are no marks, just imagine... Henry VIII must have stood right here."

Daniel's eyes lit up, a spark of recognition igniting in his expression. "Of course!" he exclaimed, his voice suddenly charged with energy. "This is where Henry stood when the Mary Rose sank."

Sophie and Claire both looked at him, intrigued by the shift in his tone.

Daniel continued, his voice taking on the familiar cadence of a historian. "It was July 19th, 1545. The French fleet was approaching, and Henry VIII came to Southsea Castle to watch his warships prepare for battle. The Mary Rose, his prized vessel, was leading the charge. But something went wrong. As she turned to engage the enemy, a gust of wind hit her sails at the wrong moment. She leaned heavily, water rushed in through the open gun ports, and within minutes, she sank right there, in full view of the king."

Claire frowned. "But what does that have to do with the treasure? Thomas' letter pointed us to Southsea Castle, but we haven't found anything."

Daniel sighed, his gaze moving from the ramparts to the sea. "I'm starting to think that Thomas' clue was meant to be physical, something that may have been lost with all the modifications to the castle over the centuries. But Edmund's letter... his clue might be something else."

Sophie straightened, her expression thoughtful. "The sixth rose," she murmured. "You don't think it could have anything to do with the Mary Rose, do you?"

Daniel nodded slowly, the pieces starting to come together in his mind. "It makes sense. The Mary Rose was Henry's pride, his 'sixth rose,' in a way. And the ship's been raised from the seabed—there's an entire museum dedicated to it now. Maybe the answer to the 'sixth rose' is there."

Sophie's eyes widened. "The Mary Rose Museum?"

Daniel smiled faintly. "Exactly. It's possible the clue we're looking for isn't here in Southsea Castle, but there, in the museum. If Edmund's clue is tied to the history of the Mary Rose, then that's where we might find the next piece of the puzzle."

Claire crossed her arms, still pondering. "So, we've come all this way, but the answer might be somewhere else entirely?"

Daniel nodded. "Maybe the clues are spread out across different places. That would make sense, especially if they're tied to important events in Portsmouth's history. The Mary

Rose is part of that history—and now it feels like we're becoming a part of it too."

Sophie glanced at Claire. "It's worth a shot. We've followed every lead here, and we've come up empty. But the Mary Rose might hold the key to the 'sixth rose.'"

Claire considered this for a moment, then gave a short nod. She'd started off seeing Daniel as just a means to an end, but his dedication and depth of knowledge were beginning to make her see him differently. "Alright. The Mary Rose Museum it is. Let's hope we're right this time."

Chapter 17

The gates of Portsmouth's Historic Dockyard loomed ahead as Daniel, Sophie, and Claire walked side by side, their footsteps echoing softly on the cobblestones beneath them. As they passed through, the towering masts of HMS Victory came into view, dominating the dockyard and casting long shadows across their path. The historic significance of their surroundings was unmistakable, and with every step, the gravity of their search seemed to intensify.

Sophie's eyes lit up as she spotted the massive aircraft carrier docked nearby. "Isn't that the HMS Queen Elizabeth we saw from the Round Tower? She's even bigger up close!"

Daniel nodded, a hint of admiration in his expression. "That's right. She's an absolute giant, the Royal Navy's flagship aircraft carrier. A real feat of modern engineering."

Sophie, ever curious, glanced at him. "How many ships have been called Queen Elizabeth?"

Daniel smiled, thinking for a moment. "There's been more than one. The first was a battleship launched in 1913 during World War I, and now we've got this one, launched just a few years ago. Both ships named after the queen, both serving different eras."

Claire, however, seemed less interested in naval trivia. Her gaze was fixed ahead, eager to move on. "As fascinating as all this is, we've got a museum to get to. Let's keep going."

Daniel gestured towards the *Victory*, his voice tinged with reverence. "There she is—*HMS Victory*. Nelson's flagship at Trafalgar." He turned to Sophie, his tone softening. "A ship like this evolved from the types of vessels that Edmund and Thomas would have commanded. Powerful, fast, heavily armed."

Sophie looked up at the *Victory's* towering masts, her eyes wide with wonder. "So Edmund's ship would have been a bit like this?"

Before Daniel could respond, Claire stepped forward, her voice precise and informed, carrying the authority of her research. "Not quite. Edmund and Thomas commanded an Intrepid-class fourth-rate frigate, HMS *Endeavour*. Smaller than *Victory*, but still formidable. Fifty guns, built for speed and versatility in battle. Their missions took them to the Caribbean, but it was their final voyage in the Mediterranean in 1709 that sealed their fates."

Daniel stopped mid-step, the word *fate* hanging heavily in the air. He blinked, his gaze shifting slowly from the *Victory* to Claire. His mouth opened as if to speak, but no words came.

Claire continued, her knowledge flowing with the ease of someone who had spent years researching every detail. "The Mediterranean was a critical battleground in the early 18th century, with the English protecting shipping routes from privateers and Spanish warships. Gibraltar was key—a gateway between Europe and the empire. Edmund and Thomas were there, not just protecting trade but disrupting Spanish operations wherever possible."

"They were sent to the Mediterranean in 1709 to protect English shipping interests near Gibraltar, and to disrupt Spanish privateers. But near Cartagena, the Spanish fleet caught them in a pincer movement. *HMS Endeavour* fought hard, but they were outnumbered and outgunned. She went down with all hands. No survivors."

Sophie's expression faltered as Claire's words sank in. Her eyes widened, and she turned sharply to her father, the realisation hitting her. "All hands?" she whispered, her voice barely audible.

Claire nodded solemnly. "None survived."

An uneasy stillness gathered around them, the impact of the revelation lingering. Daniel, usually quick with answers, remained silent, processing. Edmund's death had always been a historical fact, a distant certainty, but hearing the specifics of how his ancestor met his end made it feel startlingly real. For the first time, the stories he had studied all his life seemed to reach out, bridging the gap between past and present, turning history into something deeply personal.

"They never made it back," Sophie murmured, her voice trembling slightly. "He never came home."

Daniel swallowed hard, his throat dry. "No," his voice catching slightly as he spoke. "He didn't." He glanced down at the letter tucked safely in Sophie's bag. "He wrote that letter knowing this might happen. Knowing that the only way we'd ever know where to find the treasure would be if he didn't survive." He looked back at Claire, a new sense of responsibility settling heavily over him. "He understood the risks. And still…"

Sophie's fingers tightened around the strap of her bag, her nails digging into her palms as she clenched it harder. "It makes it feel... closer, doesn't it?" looking up at the *Victory* as if seeing it through Edmund's eyes. "Like we're really following in his footsteps. It's not just a story anymore—it's real. *He* was real."

Daniel nodded slowly, his thoughts swirling. "They weren't just thinking of treasure," his voice raw with emotion. "They were thinking of us. Their families. This letter—it's not just a map. It's a message to the future. A way of reaching out, ensuring that even if they were lost, their legacy wouldn't be."

Sophie blinked back the sting of tears, the connection to her long-dead ancestor suddenly more tangible than ever before. "He must have been scared," she whispered. "Knowing that they were sailing into something they might not come back from."

Daniel placed a hand on her shoulder, his grip gentle but firm. "He was a soldier, Sophie. They both were. But yes, I think he would have been afraid." He hesitated, his voice softening even further. "I think that's why he wrote the letter. To make sure, if the worst happened, we'd have a chance to finish what they started."

Claire crossed her arms, her face sombre but resolute. "And now it's up to us. They left these clues behind for a reason, so their story—and their treasure—wouldn't end with them."

As they drew nearer to the *Victory*, its immense hull gleamed under the sun, the freshly painted timbers and rigging giving the ship a renewed grandeur. But to Daniel, it was as if he could see past the new paint, past the restored decks, to the vessels of old—the ships that carried men like Edmund and Thomas to their final battles. The ship stood as a testament to the Royal Navy's evolution, and yet to Daniel, it now symbolised something far deeper: the lifeline Edmund and

Thomas had clung to, severed by war and time, but kept alive by their letters.

Daniel's eyes traced the ship's lines, lingering on the towering masts. "This ship," his voice low, carried the weight of reflection, "was born from the lessons learned from vessels like the Endeavour." The Royal Navy became stronger, more advanced, and more dominant because of those sacrifices. But for Edmund and Thomas, their ship wasn't just a tool of war—it was their lifeline. And when that lifeline was severed..." He paused, a note of grief lingering in his tone.

Sophie stared at the *Victory*, a wave of emotion washing over her. "All they had left were their letters," she whispered, "and the hope that someone would one day follow in their footsteps."

Claire, her arms still crossed, looked at the ship with a renewed intensity. "Let's just hope we're following those footsteps in the right direction."

Chapter 18

The trio moved silently from the commanding presence of HMS Victory toward the sleek, glass walls of the Mary Rose Museum. The transition was stark—the vibrant activity of the dockyard behind them faded into the cool stillness of the museum's interior. The dim lighting cast shadows over the carefully preserved hull of the Mary Rose, suspended mid-air like a phantom of the past. It loomed before them, bathed in soft, golden light, its dark, ancient timbers a reminder of the ship's long sleep beneath the sea.

For a moment, all three stood in solemn silence, letting the full impact of history wash over them.

Daniel was the first to speak, his voice quiet with reflection. "There she is," gesturing toward the ship. "We were just standing where Henry VIII watched her sink, his pride and joy, meant to be unstoppable. But one mistake, and she went down in full view of the king." He paused, his eyes fixed on the ship. "And now, after all these years... she's risen again. It's hard to believe anything could have survived, let alone something this remarkable."

Sophie looked up at the imposing hull of the Mary Rose, her gaze thoughtful. "You know, Dad, if we're talking about roses... do you think there's a connection with the War of the Roses? I mean, 'the sixth rose'—could that be tied to the number of roses or something?"

Daniel chuckled softly, appreciating her curiosity. "Not quite. The War of the Roses wasn't about individual roses like that. It was a civil war between two rival houses—Lancaster and York. The red rose symbolised the Lancastrians, and the white rose stood for the Yorkists. It was all about their claim to the throne." He paused, his gaze drifting toward the shipwreck. "It went on for years, bloody and brutal, until Henry Tudor—who became Henry VII—married Elizabeth of York. That's when the fighting finally stopped, and the two houses were united. The red and white together became the Tudor rose, a symbol of peace and unity."

Sophie tilted her head thoughtfully. "So, nothing to do with actual numbers of roses?"

Daniel shook his head. "No, the 'roses' in that war weren't about numbers. But the symbol of the rose has always been powerful in England, representing royalty, legitimacy, and endurance. It's a deep part of our history, but I'm not sure it links directly to what we're chasing just yet."

Sophie stared up at the impressive wooden remains, her fascination unmistakable. "Do you think this has something to do with the sixth rose?" she asked, hope threading through her voice. "The name, the ship, the fact it was lost so close to Portsmouth… it has to mean something."

Daniel's eyes swept over the relics and artifacts displayed around the hull, but before he could respond, Claire, ever pragmatic, stepped forward.

Claire's voice was steady but sceptical. "The Mary Rose is a marvel of history, no doubt. But Edmund wouldn't have known anything about it. The ship sank nearly 200 years before his time. We're chasing something too symbolic here. The Mary

Rose might have been a symbol of England's naval power, but it's not going to lead us to the treasure."

Daniel's expression shifted as he took in her words, the flicker of excitement he'd felt starting to fade. She was right. He wanted this ship to be part of the puzzle, but the dates just didn't match. The ship's name, though evocative, was nothing more than a distraction.

He nodded slowly. "You're right," he admitted. "Edmund couldn't have known about this ship, much less tied his clues to it. The Mary Rose was only discovered a few decades ago. It doesn't fit."

Sophie, standing amidst the centuries-old relics, felt a flicker of disappointment. She turned toward a display of longbows recovered from the wreckage, her fingers tracing the glass case. "Then why mention a rose at all? The sixth rose—it has to mean something, right?"

Daniel paused, reflecting on how this mystery had pulled them deeper into history than they could have imagined. He had wanted answers, not metaphors. But maybe that was where his mistake lay—perhaps the sixth rose wasn't just about a ship, or a dynasty, but something real, waiting to be uncovered.

Daniel's expression softened as he considered the deeper meaning. "It could be more metaphorical," he suggested. "A symbol of the Tudor dynasty, maybe—something that represents England's resilience. The rose has long been a symbol of the country's endurance and power. But if Claire's right, and I think she is, Edmund wasn't pointing us to this ship. His clues are leading us somewhere else."

Claire crossed her arms and glanced at the preserved wreck. "We've been thinking too much in terms of symbols and ships.

Edmund wasn't writing some cryptic riddle; he was leaving a trail—a practical, physical trail. He knew that if he didn't return, his family would need something solid to follow, not abstract ideas."

Sophie nodded, though the frustration was clear on her face. The pieces were still elusive, the path ahead blurred. She had hoped that the connection to the 'sixth rose' would yield something more tangible. But standing here, in front of the ancient timbers of the Mary Rose, the treasure felt further away than ever.

Daniel looked at her, sensing her disappointment. He understood how invested she'd become, feeling as if they were chasing shadows. "This isn't the end of the road, Soph," he said softly. "We've been following the clues, and while this may not be it, we're still moving in the right direction. The sixth rose... it has to refer to something real. Something that ties into the world Edmund knew."

Claire, her eyes scanning the exhibits one last time, nodded in agreement. "We're not far off. But we need to focus on the facts. Edmund and Thomas were practical men. They hid their treasure with the intention of it being found—by us. That means the clues will lead us to something tangible, something we can follow."

They stood together, gazing at the wreck of the Mary Rose, not in defeat, but in renewed determination. The next step was still out there, waiting to be discovered.

They moved silently through the exhibits, their eyes flitting over the array of artefacts recovered from the depths of the Solent. Cannons, navigational instruments, personal items once held by the hands of sailors long gone—each relic was a glimpse into the past, but none of it seemed to offer the connection they sought. No sign of the sixth rose, no clear path to the treasure.

They came to a stop in front of a mural depicting the final moments of the *Mary Rose*. The scene was vivid—Henry VIII on horseback in front of Southsea Castle, his figure tall and commanding, though his gaze wasn't fixed on the disaster unfolding at sea. Instead, he seemed to be riding as if oblivious to the sinking warship behind him.

Claire's gaze lingered on the king, resplendent in his royal finery, sitting tall on his horse. "Why show him like this?" she asked, her voice sceptical. "He's not even looking at the ship. Wasn't he supposed to be watching when it happened?"

Daniel stepped closer to the mural, his expression thoughtful. "Well, it's complicated. We know he was at Southsea Castle when the *Mary Rose* sank—he was there to observe the battle. But whether or not he was literally watching when the ship went down, no one really knows. This kind of image... it's more symbolic than factual."

Sophie glanced up at the mural. "So, it's not meant to show what really happened?"

"Not exactly," Daniel let out a sigh. "It's more about portraying Henry's power. Even in moments of failure, they paint him on horseback, as if he's in control. But in reality, he couldn't do a thing to stop the *Mary Rose* from sinking. The ship was lost before anyone could intervene."

Claire nodded slowly, her eyes still on the mural. "I guess it just shows how much history gets romanticised. The king on horseback, in front of his castle, while his greatest ship is going down behind him."

Daniel's gaze drifted back to the mural. "Exactly. But despite the story, I think we're barking up the wrong tree here," he muttered, shaking his head. "The *Mary Rose*—it's just not our sixth rose."

Sophie glanced at the remains of the hull behind them, its fragmented timbers reaching into the dim light of the museum. A frown creased her brow, disappointment tugging at her.

"Then why did we come here?" she asked, her voice tinged with frustration.

Claire, ever pragmatic, stepped in, her tone steady and unfazed. "Because we had to rule it out. That's part of this process. We're following clues, but not every lead is going to take us where we expect. This was just one of the paths we had to explore."

Sophie's gaze lingered on the wreck of the Mary Rose, standing before them like a silent testament to history. It felt as though they were brushing against something significant, yet still just out of reach of what they were truly seeking.

Daniel's jaw tightened, his determination undimmed. "Every lead teaches us something, even if it leads to a dead end." The words were firm, almost as if meant to convince himself. "We'll keep going. The sixth rose is still out there, somewhere. This wasn't it, but it's not the end of the trail."

Emerging from the Mary Rose Museum, the chill in the air hit sharply, wrapping around them as they stepped into the brightness outside. Nearby, HMS Victory rose into the sky, her masts cutting through the light with a commanding presence. The hull seemed to glow under the afternoon sun, its polished surface standing in stark contrast to the lengthening shadows stretching across the dockyard. Sophie's gaze lingered on the rigging for a moment, but the ship's grandeur only deepened the frustration she felt—an unspoken tension clinging to the cool air, as though the past refused to fully give up its mysteries.

"Well, that didn't exactly lead us anywhere," Sophie muttered, her sigh almost lost in the hum of the dockyard's crowd.

Daniel remained quiet beside her, clearly lost in thought, his mind still sifting through the fragments of the day's findings. Claire, however, strode ahead with her usual confidence, seemingly unperturbed by their lack of progress.

Amid the bustling crowd of dockyard visitors, Sophie caught sight of Claire near the massive anchor in the courtyard. She was speaking quietly with a man who looked vaguely familiar, their conversation brief and muted amidst the noise of the passing crowd. Suspicion stirred in Sophie's mind, but before she could act on it, Claire returned to their group, her expression composed and her smile effortlessly casual.

Daniel noticed Sophie's slight frown and glanced at Claire. "Who was that?"

Claire waved it off, her smile easy. "Oh, just another visitor. We were just chatting about how amazing the museum is. Can't help but get caught up in the history."

Sophie's unease didn't vanish, but she kept quiet, making a mental note of the exchange.

Daniel, however, remained oblivious, still preoccupied with their progress—or lack thereof. "Henry VIII and his wives, though," Claire began, her voice laced with irony. "There's always a story with them. Poor women losing their heads because of his whims."

Sophie shot her a look, a mix of irritation and disbelief. "Not all of them lost their heads, you know."

Claire shrugged, her grin playful. "Close enough. The man went through wives like ships passing in the night. Relentless, wasn't he?"

A faint smile tugged at Sophie's lips despite herself, but she wasn't about to let Claire get away with the oversimplification. "Actually, the rhyme goes, 'Divorced, beheaded, died, divorced, beheaded, survived.' Catherine Parr—she's the one who survived."

Daniel stopped dead in his tracks, turning to face them with an intensity that sent a ripple of surprise through the group. His eyes widened, his mind suddenly racing. "Six wives..." he muttered, more to himself than to them. "Six English roses... and one survived."

Sophie blinked, her confusion evident. "Dad?"

Daniel's thoughts were moving faster than he could articulate. The pieces of the puzzle were falling into place in his mind. He glanced at Sophie, his eyes shining with realisation.

"Six wives," he repeated, his voice gaining strength. "Six Tudor roses. Catherine Parr—she's the sixth rose!"

Claire's interest sharpened immediately, her eyes narrowing as she processed his sudden shift. "Catherine Parr?" she asked, her tone cautious but intrigued. "What are you getting at?"

Without missing a beat, Sophie fumbled in her bag, pulling out Edmund's letter with trembling fingers. She unfolded the parchment, her breath quickening as she laid it out before them. Daniel's eyes scanned the familiar lines, but now, they gleamed with newfound clarity. His finger hovered over the passage that had haunted them for days.

"The sixth rose…" Daniel read aloud, his voice firm. "'The sixth rose, a bridge too far, guards the secret, an arch scar.'"

He looked up at them, his voice steady as the realisation took hold. "It's Catherine Parr. She's the sixth rose. There's a bridge near Titchfield Abbey, where she lived after Henry VIII's death. The Abbey became Place House after the Dissolution of the Monasteries, reinforcing its royal connections. The bridge was once called Anjou Bridge, named after Margaret of Anjou, wife of Henry VI, who visited Titchfield Abbey in 1445 for the reconfirmation of her marriage. Now known as Stony Bridge, it links both Catherine and Margaret—two queens connected to this place. That's the bridge Edmund's letter is referring to."

"Sophie's heart raced as the revelation settled in. "So… the sixth rose isn't just a metaphor," her voice rising with excitement. "It's Catherine Parr! And that bridge is our next clue!"

Claire's eyes flashed with understanding, her expression shifting from curiosity to determination. She reached into her jacket pocket, pulling out her own letter. Quickly unfolding it, she scanned the lines, her voice growing more certain as she read.

"When the sea turns to land and the tides no longer call, seek where time has swallowed the truth. Beyond the bend, where the river meets the earth, a bridge of stone will guide your way."

Sophie and Daniel exchanged a stunned look.

"Both letters…" Sophie's voice carried a note of awe as her eyes widened. "They're talking about the same bridge."

Claire nodded, her excitement barely contained. "That's what it's all been pointing to—my letter, your letter. They've both been leading us to Titchfield Abbey's stone bridge, and its connection to Catherine Parr."

Daniel folded Edmund's letter with deliberate care, his expression a blend of determination and anticipation. "We need to go to Titchfield Abbey." His tone was firm. "The sixth rose is Catherine Parr, and that bridge—that's our next step."

Sophie chuckled, her eyes sparkling with humour. "So, the path ahead looks... rosie?" She glanced at Claire, who raised an eyebrow before cracking a smile.

Claire tucked her letter away, ready to follow this new lead. "Alright, let's not waste any time. Titchfield Abbey and the bridge... this could be it. But let's stay sharp—we might still be missing something."

As they stood there in the shadow of history—HMS Victory behind them and Titchfield Abbey ahead—the sense of discovery was almost overwhelming. Two families, two letters, one legacy. And now, after centuries of mystery, the pieces were finally coming together. With renewed determination, they set off toward the next chapter of their journey—toward the stone bridge near Titchfield Abbey, where the secrets of the past lay waiting to be uncovered.

Chapter 19

5th November 1708 – Coast of England.

The night air hung heavy with tension as HMS *Endeavour* sat motionless in the dark waters just off the coast. The once-proud ship, her sails furled and her crew settled into uneasy silence, seemed to merge with the gloom of the moonless night. On the deck, Edmund Grey stood with Captain Hastings, their faces grim, watching as the small boat was lowered into the inky blackness below.

The soft creak of the ropes and the faint splash of the boat hitting the water were the only sounds that broke the stillness. Thomas' voice, low and urgent, pierced the quiet.

"Make it quick, Edmund. The fewer eyes on this, the better."

Edmund nodded, his jaw set in determination. "It'll be done. They believe it's just rum."

Below them, Harper, Briggs, and Ward—Edmund's trusted men—waited in the boat, eyes averted from their superiors. The barrels, which were carefully lowered down to them, felt heavier with each passing minute, their weight not only physical but symbolic of the secrets they carried. The men's muscles strained under the burden, grunting quietly as they adjusted the load. The air felt close and oppressive, as though the tension of the night and their mission pressed down on them.

As Edmund climbed down into the boat, the crew adjusted the barrels, grunting under their weight.

Harper whispered to Briggs, "Strange time to be shifting rum, don't you think?"

Briggs shrugged, glancing towards the looming shadows of the shore. "Aye, but it's not our place to ask questions."

Edmund caught their hushed conversation and shot them a sharp, warning glance. "Keep your voices down." His tone was icy, his eyes flashing with intensity. "We've work to do."

Thomas, still on deck, nodded once more to Edmund as the boat began to drift away. His voice was barely more than a murmur as he watched them disappear into the darkness. "Godspeed, Edmund."

The small boat cut silently through the water, the rhythmic splash of the oars the only sound as they navigated the narrow canal. The tall trees lining the banks loomed darkly, and the occasional rustling in the underbrush only served to heighten the tension among the men. The canal, narrow and winding, stretched out ahead of them like a tunnel of secrets, leading them deeper into the unknown.

Edmund sat at the helm, eyes fixed forward, his mind a swirl of conflicting thoughts. Each stroke of the oars brought them closer to their destination, and with every pull, the creak of the wood seemed louder, more ominous. The men rowed hard, their arms burning from the strain, the tension between them as taut as the ropes securing their cargo.

Ward, always the nervy one, broke the silence, his voice trembling slightly. "Feels like we're heading straight for the devil's own doorstep."

Edmund's eyes remained fixed ahead. "Keep rowing. We've a job to do."

As they rounded a bend in the canal, a faint orange glow appeared on the horizon, illuminating the distant treetops with an unsettling flicker. The men paused, gazing at the glow with wary curiosity. Briggs was the first to voice what they all were wondering, "What in the devil's name is that?"

Harper squinted, realization dawning. "Bonfires... It's Guy Fawkes Night, isn't it?"

Edmund's gaze hardened, an uneasy feeling creeping over him. He thought of Guy Fawkes, the infamous traitor, and found an uncomfortable parallel to his own actions tonight. How had they overlooked this night of all nights in their planning? The irony was not lost on him—their secretive mission now mirrored Fawkes' failed scheme to conceal a dangerous cargo under cover of darkness. The risk they faced tonight felt amplified, the glow of distant fires a reminder of treachery and consequences.

Ward, nervously tugging at his collar, added, "Hope those fires don't bring unwelcome eyes our way."

Edmund's voice was gruff as he ordered, "Keep rowing. We're losing time." But deep down, an unsettling significance to the night stayed with him.

As they continued, the rhythmic thrum of a watermill came into focus. The mill loomed ahead, its great wooden wheel turning lazily in the night, dipping into the water with a steady creak. The sight of it was almost hypnotic—a reminder that time marched on, indifferent to the secrets they carried.

Briggs, staring at the mill as they passed, muttered, "That wheel's been turning for as long as I can remember. Who knows what it's seen?"

Edmund, his voice low and steely, responded without turning. "Eyes forward. We're not here to marvel at old stones."

Yet the sight of the watermill stuck with Edmund. The slow, deliberate turning of the wheel reminded him of the inevitability of time—the same force that could either reveal their treasure to the world or bury it forever in forgotten history. Time moved on, whether they succeeded or failed, just like that mill turning tirelessly, seeing countless nights like this.

As the boat glided deeper into the canal, a shadowy structure emerged from the darkness ahead—the bridge. Built of ancient stone, its low arches spanned the narrow waterway, moss clinging to its sides like a forgotten relic of the past. It seemed to breathe history, its weathered surface glowing faintly in the dim light of the moon.

"There it is," Edmund whispered. "The bridge."

The men rowed silently beneath one arch, their faces tense, the sound of the oars now eerily muffled by the stone structure above them. As the boat came to a stop, Edmund was the first to leap out, boots sinking slightly into the soft earth as he landed on the bank.

One by one, the barrels were carefully lifted from the boat and placed beneath the bridge, concealed in a small alcove where the shadows were deepest. The stone, jagged and sharp in places, scraped against their hands as they worked. The distant hoot of an owl broke the silence, sending a shiver through the group. The men, breathless from their efforts, exchanged uneasy glances.

Harper, his voice a low mutter, could no longer contain his suspicion. "Feels like we're shifting more than rum." His thoughts drifted to Guy Fawkes and the barrels of gunpowder smuggled beneath the Houses of Parliament all those years ago.

Edmund's expression darkened, his voice barely more than a growl. "Mind your tongue, Harper. What we carry tonight isn't for idle speculation."

As they secured the last barrel, a faint glow appeared above them. Edmund's breath hitched as torchlight reflected in the water, stretching in eerie ripples across the river's surface. A small group of figures moved across the bridge, their voices low but close enough to carry in the stillness.

The men below huddled in silence, pressing into the shadows, each one holding their breath. The torches bobbed overhead, casting fleeting beams down to the water, lighting the stones where the barrels now lay hidden. The flickering glow inched across Edmund's face before passing on, leaving them momentarily shrouded in darkness once more.

But as the voices drifted away, Edmund's heart continued to race, knowing full well they weren't out of danger yet. Every sound felt amplified, every rustle a potential threat. If they made the slightest noise now, it could undo everything.

Chapter 20

The engine hummed softly as Claire gripped the wheel, her gaze fixed ahead in unwavering concentration. In the back seat, maps and documents lay scattered, some crumpled, others marked with hurried notes. Her drone case, mud-splattered from her recent search at Fareham Creek, sat wedged tightly between the seats—a silent testament to her meticulous, almost relentless pursuit.

Sophie glanced at Claire, noticing the intensity in her posture. This was more than a treasure hunt for her; it felt personal, like a quest she was determined to see through at any cost. The car's interior, from the crumpled papers to the tossed coffee cups, bore the signs of Claire's single-minded focus. Sophie felt a flicker of admiration but also a hint of caution—she wasn't sure if they were following the clues or if Claire's ambition was driving them instead.

As she drove, Claire's mind swirled with conflicting thoughts. She had been so certain her methods would yield results—so sure that Fareham Creek held the answers. But doubt crept in, a slow, insidious voice in the back of her mind. What if she was wrong? What if the treasure wasn't there, after all? And worse still, what if she had been leading Daniel and Sophie astray, wasting their time? Her reputation, her very purpose in this hunt, felt like it was hanging by a thread.

Claire sighed, leaning back slightly before turning to Daniel and Sophie. "Look, before we rush off to Titchfield Abbey, maybe we should take a breath. We've been at this all day, and I'm not entirely convinced yet," she admitted, shifting in her seat. Her foot tapped against the pedal, a sign of her restlessness.

Sophie looked up from her phone, while Daniel gave her a quizzical glance. "What's holding you back?" he asked, though his voice wasn't confrontational—more curious than anything.

Before Claire could respond, a car suddenly swerved into their lane, forcing her to brake hard. "Are you kidding me?" she snapped, her hands tightening around the wheel as she cursed under her breath. "Some people shouldn't be allowed to drive," she muttered, shaking her head, her irritation bubbling to the surface.

"Maybe we should take a break," Daniel said lightly, suppressing a smirk. He wasn't used to seeing Claire lose her cool so easily. It was clear that the stress of the hunt—and possibly the lingering doubt—was starting to get to her.

Claire took a deep breath, regaining her composure. "Yeah. There's a pub on the way—The Mill, in Fareham. It's not far from here, and it'll give us a chance to regroup. We can grab some tea and really look at these letters again before we go charging off to Titchfield."

Daniel nodded, glancing at Sophie, who shrugged in agreement. "Sounds like a plan. Let's take a moment to clear our heads."

Claire shifted the car back into gear and pulled into traffic more calmly this time, her earlier tension fading as she headed toward The Mill Pub.

As they pulled into the gravel driveway of The Mill, the warm glow of lights spilling from the pub's windows brought an instant sense of comfort. Inside, the low hum of conversation mixed with the smell of wood smoke and the comforting aroma of freshly cooked food. It felt like stepping into a different world—one far removed from the pressure of their search.

The comforting warmth of the pub filled the room as they settled into a quiet table by the window, a pot of tea and a plate of freshly baked scones between them. Claire spread out her letter on the table, her finger running over the passage she'd been puzzling over.

Sophie leaned back in her chair, the tension in her shoulders finally easing. She had been glued to her phone for most of the day, tracking their progress, checking maps, and looking for connections. But now, sitting in the cosy pub, she couldn't help but let her mind wander. How had they come this far? A few days ago, they were just following a hunch, and now it felt like they were on the cusp of something much bigger. Yet, that sense of elation was laced with exhaustion—and the nagging fear that maybe they were missing something crucial.

"It's this line here," Claire began, tapping the paper, "'When the sea turns to land and the tides no longer call, seek where time has swallowed the truth.' That has to be talking about Fareham Creek. The tides come in, but they don't go very far anymore. I've searched the area pretty thoroughly, though." She chuckled, shaking her head. "Found an old wheelbarrow yesterday, but no treasure yet."

Daniel smiled, glancing out the window as Claire continued. "And the next part—'Follow the waters beyond, where the land surrenders to the pull of the sea'—could be somewhere further up the River Wallington, which starts right here." She pointed out the window toward the bridge visible in the distance. "Look there, a bridge of stone guiding the way."

Daniel turned his head to the view, considering it for a moment. "That bridge looks like it was built in the 19th century, made of red brick, not stone. It's a railway viaduct—probably not what Thomas would've meant."

Claire raised an eyebrow. "But that doesn't mean there wasn't a bridge here before, right? Places change, just like Southsea Castle."

"True," Daniel acknowledged, "but look at the first part of the letter: 'When the sea turns to land and the tides no longer call.' That fits perfectly with the history of the River Meon. It used to be a tidal estuary, and ships could sail right up to Titchfield, which was a significant port at the time. But in the 16th century, the Earl of Southampton drained the river to make Southampton a more important port. It crippled Titchfield's status. The tides don't call there anymore."

Claire frowned, her fingers drumming on the table. "So you think this line is more about the River Meon, not Fareham Creek?"

"Exactly." Daniel's tone was measured, his mind working through the possibilities. "Thomas would've known the river's history. Maybe ships couldn't go up it after it was drained, but a small boat with a crew could still navigate parts of it. That line—'When the sea turns to land'—it's referring to a place that used to be ruled by the tides but isn't anymore."

Sophie, who had been looking at her phone, chimed in. "Dad's right. I checked some old maps, and the Meon used to be much bigger. It was a major estuary, but after the Earl drained it, it became less navigable. This canal here," she pointed at her phone, "drained the water out, leaving Titchfield to fade as a port."

Claire leaned back, her eyes narrowing in thought. "Okay, but what about the bridge? Thomas mentioned 'a bridge of stone.'"

"That could be referring to the bridge at Titchfield Abbey," Daniel suggested. "It's older than the railway viaduct here, and given the importance of Titchfield as a port before the Earl's changes, it makes sense that Thomas would reference that stone bridge."

Claire toyed with her scone, absentmindedly spreading the cream first before adding the jam. "I see what you're saying. Maybe I've been too focused on what's right in front of me instead of thinking about how things used to be."

Daniel, who had spread jam first on his scone, raised an eyebrow. "Jam first? You've been doing it all wrong."

Claire rolled her eyes. "Please, cream goes on first."

Sophie smiled, watching the back-and-forth. "And we're debating scones while hunting for treasure…"

Sophie looked out the window, letting the conversation wash over her. The hunt, the constant drive forward—it had been exhilarating. But moments like this, where they could breathe, made her realise how much they'd already uncovered. Her fingers traced the edge of her phone, an idle thought flickering in her mind: they were on the brink of something monumental, but the fear of misinterpreting the clues haunted her. Was Titchfield Abbey really their answer?

Claire sighed, setting her scone down. "Alright, I'll admit it—this Titchfield Abbey theory of yours is starting to fit. Maybe I was too focused on Fareham Creek."

Daniel smiled, sensing her shift. "So we're headed to Titchfield Abbey?"

Claire nodded. "Yeah, let's give it a shot. I think we might actually be onto something."

She leaned back and smirked. "Though, honestly, wouldn't it have been easier if Thomas and Grey had just drawn us a map with a big X marking the spot?"

Daniel chuckled, shaking his head. "Then where's the fun in that?"

Chapter 21

The narrow road sloped gently downhill, leading toward the River Meon, its path winding through the quiet, pastoral beauty of the Hampshire countryside. Claire guided the car into a small pull-off, a gravelled area beside a cattle gate that opened onto a grassy field dotted with milk cows. The car rolled to a halt, its engine cutting out, leaving only the soft murmur of wind and the distant sound of the river below.

Stepping out, Claire took a long look at the scene before her. She pulled out her phone and quickly typed: "Thx 4 all ur help. I got it from here." With a brief sigh of relief, she pocketed the phone and turned her focus back to the bridge.

The bridge, with its two simple stone arches, lay at the bottom of the slope, its timeworn surface blending into the landscape as if it had always been there. Beyond it, the ruins of Titchfield Abbey stood like a silent guardian, watching over the centuries. There was no road sign or modern marker, just the road, the bridge, and the Abbey—hidden in plain sight, waiting.

This was it. The moment she had pictured countless times, pouring over maps and deciphering letters. But now, standing here at last, Claire felt the full gravity of it settle on her. The reality was a strange combination of triumph and uncertainty—triumph that they were so close, and uncertainty about what would happen if they were wrong.

Sophie climbed out of the car next, her gaze immediately drawn downhill to the bridge. The road dipped towards the river, narrowing as it approached the ancient stone structure. The soft murmur of the water could just be heard, mingling with the rustling leaves in the wind.

Sophie's eyes widened as she took in the scene. "That's it, isn't it?" she murmured, more to herself than anyone else, her voice catching slightly on the words.

Claire's gaze lingered on the worn stones. She exhaled slowly. "Yeah." Her tone was quiet, almost as if she needed the confirmation herself. "That's it—the bridge Catherine Parr would have crossed." A faint tremor laced her voice, the reality of the moment settling over her. Every step of their journey had brought them to this point.

Daniel joined them, his breath catching slightly as he took in the view. He reached up, absently rubbing the back of his neck—a gesture he often made when absorbing a revelation. "This road." His voice dropped to a near whisper, heavy with awe. "Catherine Parr would have travelled this very path, walked down this hill, and crossed that bridge on her way to the Abbey."

As they moved closer, Sophie noticed something in Claire's stance—a shift in her usual self-assurance, a rare vulnerability. She had always been so methodical, so sure of her steps. Now, for the first time, it seemed the importance of the moment was affecting her too.

Together, they started down the narrow road. The grassy fields stretched out to their left, milk cows grazing lazily in the warm afternoon sun. To their right, the River Meon curved gently toward the bridge, its waters clear and calm. With each step, the Abbey came closer into view—its crumbling stone walls standing in stark contrast to the tranquil countryside.

"It's incredible to think," Sophie said, her voice soft with wonder, "that Catherine Parr would have crossed this very bridge. How many times did she walk this road?"

As they neared the base of the hill, the bridge loomed ahead, its ancient stones weathered but strong. The River Meon flowed quietly beneath it, its gentle current whispering as it passed. The bridge itself was simple, unadorned, and yet there was something undeniably majestic about it—a connection to the past that made it more than just a span of stone over water.

Claire paused at the edge of the bridge, her eyes scanning its worn surface. "This is where it begins." The words came quietly, the presence of history settling heavily around her.

Sophie stepped closer, looking from the bridge to the Abbey, its weathered ruins just a stone's throw away, almost within reach. "What are we supposed to find here?" she asked, her voice tinged with both excitement and apprehension.

"We'll know when we find it," Daniel replied, his eyes scanning the ancient stones. "The bridge guards the secret, just like the letters said. We just have to figure out how."

With a fresh sense of purpose, they crossed the bridge, their footsteps barely audible over the soft whisper of the river below. Somewhere within the stones lay the key to a centuries-old mystery, one that their ancestors had left behind, waiting for them to uncover.

Daniel, Sophie, and Claire stood atop the Abbey Bridge, eyes scanning the weathered stone, fingers grazing the cool surface in a desperate search for the elusive clue. Below, the River Meon flowed steadily, the soft sounds of water mingling with the occasional rustle of leaves in the breeze. Despite the tranquillity around them, the tension in the air was palpable.

Daniel leaned over the edge, his movements tense with focus. "It has to be here somewhere," he muttered, frustration creeping into his voice. "Another engraving, perhaps. Like the 'G' at The Round Tower—maybe it's an 'H' this time."

Sophie, standing on the opposite side of the bridge, let her gaze drift over the ancient stones. Her arms crossed tightly, and a trace of impatience flickered in her voice. "We're missing something. This can't be a dead end."

Suddenly, the distant rumble of an approaching car broke the quiet. Daniel straightened, turning to glance up the narrow road. "We'll need to move."

The bridge was old, narrow—too narrow for both pedestrians and vehicles. The three of them quickly shuffled into a small stone refuge built into the side of the bridge, a recessed alcove barely large enough for them to stand side by side. The stone was rough and worn smooth in places by centuries of use, offering just enough space for pedestrians to step aside as traffic passed by.

As a car crawled past, the driver gave a brief nod in acknowledgement, and Claire's eyes met his for a moment. It was the private investigator. Good. He understood, she thought, feeling a sense of gratitude. He did his job well. She offered him a small nod in return, appreciating his professionalism and discretion. As the car disappeared from view, she turned her focus back to the bridge, pressing against the rough stone until the sound of the engine faded.

Sophie turned to Claire, an idea lighting up her face. "What about your drone?" she asked, her voice carrying a note of excitement. "If we can't see anything from up here, it might be on the sides, or even underneath."

Claire, always prepared, gave a quick nod. "Good thinking." She moved swiftly back up the hill towards her car to retrieve the drone. Daniel and Sophie remained on the bridge, still scouring the stones, trying to make sense of the puzzle.

Moments later, Claire returned with the drone in hand. She powered it up, and with a soft hum, the machine lifted into the air, hovering above them. She expertly guided it along the edges of the bridge, its camera zooming in on every crack and crevice.

Sophie watched the drone with bated breath. "See anything yet?"

Claire shook her head, her eyes fixed on the live video feed from the drone. "Nothing that looks out of place."

She manoeuvred the drone lower, beneath the eastern arch now, skimming just above the water. But as she tried to angle the camera to look up at the underside of the arches, she frowned. "I can't get a good angle on it. The camera won't tilt far enough."

Daniel sighed, pushing his hands through his hair. He could already feel the cold bite of the water against his bare skin in his mind, dreading the thought of wading in. "Looks like we'll have to get a closer look ourselves."

Claire didn't hesitate. "I'll need to get my waders on," she said, already moving toward the riverbank where she could gear up.

As Claire adjusted her waders and prepared to wade into the water, Daniel couldn't help but be struck by how she looked in this moment—practical yet oddly graceful. She was back in her fishing waders, just like that first time they had seen her on the beach at the Round Tower, and yet now, there was something undeniably attractive about her focus, her determination. He'd never admit it, not aloud, but there was something about Claire's rugged efficiency that drew him in, and he found himself watching her with new eyes.

Minutes later, Claire was standing in the middle of the River Meon, the cold water swirling around her legs as she waded towards the eastern arch. The current was steady but gentle, allowing her to approach the underside of the bridge with care.

She searched with her hands, feeling along the stone, but found nothing. Frustration crept in as Claire searched the arch again, fingers running over every crack and crevice, but there was no sign of anything unusual. She let out a quiet sigh, shaking her head as she turned back toward the riverbank.

Sophie, watching from the edge, called out. "Anything? Maybe try feeling higher up, closer to the curve?"

Claire glanced back at her, then nodded. "Good idea. I'll give it one more go."

With renewed determination, Claire stretched upward, reaching into the cold, slick stone where the arch curved steeply. But after several more passes, there was still nothing—just smooth stone worn down by centuries of water and weather.

Undeterred, Claire moved toward the western arch. Sophie watched her closely, squinting as the light faded further beneath the stone. "Do you want me to shine a light?" Sophie offered, pulling out her phone.

"No need," Claire replied, stepping carefully through the water. "I think I've got it from here."

As she reached under the western arch, Claire's fingers grazed something carved into the surface—a series of lines, rough and uneven. Her heart skipped a beat. She paused for a moment, then carefully traced the lines again, confirming the shape beneath her fingertips.

"I've found something!" Claire's voice echoed slightly under the stone arches, carrying across the water to Daniel and Sophie.

Sophie, excitement rising, scrambled closer to the water's edge, holding up her phone to try to catch a glimpse of Claire's discovery. "What is it? What does it look like?"

Claire shifted her weight, turning to look at them with a wide grin. "It's an engraving... some sort of compass," she called, her tone filled with both excitement and disbelief. "It's pointing south."

Daniel's eyes widened, the centuries-old connection drawing around them like an invisible tether. "A compass rose," he murmured, more to himself than anyone else. It almost didn't seem real. "A compass pointing south..." he repeated, as if trying to anchor himself in the reality of the discovery.

Claire began to wade back toward the bank, the water rippling around her legs as she moved with deliberate precision. When she reached them, she handed her phone to Daniel, who examined the photo closely. The engraving was clear—a small but unmistakable compass rose, etched into the stone beneath the western arch. Its needle pointed firmly south.

Sophie leaned in, her eyes narrowing as she stared at the image. "That's it, isn't it?" she asked quietly. "From Edmund's letter—the 'arch scar.'"

Daniel's eyes flickered with recognition. "'The sixth rose, a bridge too far, guards the secret, an arch scar,'" he murmured, repeating the line from the letter. He traced the photo with his thumb, his voice steady. "This must be the scar. This compass rose is our next clue."

"It's definitely a compass rose," Daniel confirmed, showing Sophie the photo. "But why south?"

Sophie's excitement bubbled over. "Does that mean we head south from here? What's the connection?"

Claire, peeling off her waders, looked at Daniel. "South from the bridge... It's a direction, surely. Could be the next step in the trail." Her mind raced as she recalled the last line of Thomas's letter: 'a bridge of stone will guide your way.' They were standing at the very bridge Thomas had described, and it was the final clue in the letter. They had to be close—really close.

Daniel nodded, deep in thought. "The letters mentioned a path, but now it's clear—this compass is giving us a direction. South from here... that's our next move."

Sophie, unable to contain her enthusiasm, beamed. "Then we've got our next lead. South it is."

With the discovery of the compass rose bearing south, they had their next clue. The Abbey Bridge had given up its secret. Now, they would follow the compass, knowing that every step southward brought them closer to the treasure that had been hidden for centuries.

Chapter 22

The discovery of the compass rose beneath the Abbey Bridge was the breakthrough they had been waiting for. They had been piecing together fragmented clues, following the trail of Edmund Grey's letter, unsure of where it would take them next. But now, as Sophie, Daniel, and Claire stood by the river, staring at the ancient etching in the stone, they had their answer: south.

Sophie pulled out her phone with practiced efficiency, tapping quickly to open the compass app. "We need to make sure we stay on course." She glanced at Claire and Daniel, her focus unwavering. "Let's use this to track the bearing."

Claire nodded, already holding up her phone, aligning it with the stone-carved compass rose. Daniel, however, hesitated, looking beyond the bridge to the grassy field that stretched out before them, dotted with milk cows.

Sophie caught his expression and smirked. "Don't tell me you're scared of a few cows, Dad."

Daniel straightened, attempting to mask his unease. "I'm not scared. I just... respect them. They're large, unpredictable creatures."

Claire let out a soft laugh. "Come on, Daniel. They're cows, not wild beasts. You'll be fine."

Without waiting for further debate, Sophie strode into the field, weaving between the cows with ease. Claire followed, casting a teasing glance back at Daniel. Reluctantly, he brought up the rear, eyeing the herd with caution. The cows, entirely uninterested in the human trio, barely lifted their heads as they passed.

They moved carefully across the field, phones in hand, the digital compasses guiding them south. The cows, oblivious to the trio's quest, wandered lazily in the pasture, chewing thoughtfully as the humans crossed their territory. Daniel kept a wary eye on the creatures, giving them a wide berth, his discomfort evident with each hesitant step.

Claire was the first to spot it—a weathered stone, half-hidden beneath the long grass at the far edge of the field. "Here," she called out, waving Sophie and Daniel over, her voice tinged with excitement.

Sophie reached her side, kneeling down to brush the grass aside. Her fingers traced the worn edges of the stone, brushing aside tufts of green to reveal the familiar etching. "Another compass rose!" she exclaimed, her face lighting up with excitement. "It's pointing northwest this time."

Sophie checked her phone, her thumb swiping across the screen to adjust the compass. "Northwest." Her eyes lifted from the screen, locking on the path ahead. "That takes us toward the Abbey."

Claire squatted next to the stone, studying the carving intently. "It's definitely Thomas' work," she murmured. "They must've known exactly where this trail would lead."

Behind them, Daniel suddenly stopped in his tracks, an audible squelch breaking the silence. He grimaced, looking down to see his shoe planted firmly in something unpleasant.

"Careful where you step, Dad," Sophie teased, a grin spreading across her face. "Or you'll end up with more than just ancient treasure on your boots."

Daniel, his usual composed demeanour shattered for a moment, glared down at the cow pat smeared across his shoe. He shook his head in disbelief. "Wonderful. Just wonderful. Chasing treasure and dodging cow pats—this is exactly what I had in mind."

Claire chuckled, standing up and offering him a wry smile. "A small price to pay for history, don't you think?"

Daniel grumbled but couldn't help the spark of excitement returning to his eyes. He shook off the cow pat with a frustrated kick and rejoined the others. The compass rose they had found was clear: northwest, straight toward the looming silhouette of Titchfield Abbey.

They pressed on, the anticipation growing as they followed the compass bearing towards the ancient ruins. The Abbey rose before them, its skeletal walls standing against the sky, remnants of a grand past now weathered by centuries. The heavy gates creaked as they pushed through, stepping inside the grounds of the once magnificent structure.

The air here held a distinct stillness, as if layered with stories long forgotten. Daniel's gaze softened, his historian's instincts coming to life as he took in the weathered stones and crumbling walls around them.

Just inside the gate, Sophie came to an abrupt stop, her gaze locking onto a faint carving in the stonework by the entrance.

She raised her hand, pointing. "Look over there—another compass rose."

Daniel and Claire hurried over, and there, carved into the worn stone beside the gate, was the third compass rose. This one pointed west, deeper into the abbey grounds.

"Three compass roses," Daniel muttered, his excitement building. "They're leading us somewhere. This must be another step on the path."

The significance of the Abbey was undeniable. With each clue, they were moving closer—closer to uncovering the secrets left behind by their ancestors. The abbey's decayed grandeur surrounded them, and somewhere within, the next piece of the puzzle awaited.

The ruins of Titchfield Abbey stood before them, ancient and weathered, with crumbling walls and the remains of grand arches outlined against the sky. Daniel, Sophie, and Claire moved carefully through the grounds. A profound sense of history surrounded them as they walked. Daniel's gaze lingered on the stone remnants of what had once been a majestic structure, a trace of wistfulness colouring his voice.

"This place," Daniel began, his voice low but resonant, "was once a thriving abbey, founded in 1231. It housed a community of Premonstratensian monks for over three centuries. During the dissolution of the monasteries under Henry VIII's orders, the abbey was bestowed upon Sir Thomas Wriothesley, one of his trusted allies, who repurposed it into an impressive mansion.

Sophie listened closely, absorbing the details, but Claire was less concerned with the abbey's former glory. She scanned the ground, a look of unease crossing her face as she glanced around the ruins. "But now it's in ruins," she muttered, half to herself.

Daniel stopped, sensing her unease. "It is, yes. Time, neglect, and the elements have taken their toll."

Claire looked up at the crumbling arches and stone walls, her face tense with realisation. "If Thomas or Edmund left any more compass roses in these walls, they could have been lost—eroded over centuries. Not because of renovations like at Southsea Castle, but because the abbey itself is falling apart."

Sophie's face fell. "So the clues might be gone?"

Claire nodded slowly, her eyes scanning the ruined structure. "It's possible. These walls have been exposed to the weather for centuries. Any carvings could be worn down or completely lost."

Daniel sighed, sensing the depth of her concern. "It's possible," he admitted. "But we've come this far. If there's even a chance the compass roses are still here, we have to keep searching."

Determined not to lose hope, they pressed westward, their compasses guiding them toward the edge of the boundary wall. The remains of the wall jutted out ahead of them, covered in moss and ivy, but something caught Sophie's eye—another stone marker, hidden beneath the overgrowth.

"Here!" she called, pulling back the vines. A fourth compass rose was etched into the stone, pointing toward the abbey's main tower.

"Still intact," Daniel murmured with a flicker of relief. "We're still on track."

They followed the new bearing, winding their way through the ruins until they reached the shadow of the main tower wall. The structure, though damaged, still stood tall, a remnant of the abbey's former power. And there, carved into the base of the wall, was the fifth compass rose.

"This one points to the well." Claire's movements quickened, her focus shifting to the centre of the courtyard. Her breath hitched as she turned, eyes locking on the ancient stone well, weathered and silent, nestled among the remains of crumbling pillars.

As they neared the well, a sense of expectation gripped the trio. The abbey, with all its secrets and history, now felt more alive than ever—its ruins whispering ancient promises that something monumental was about to happen.

The trio moved closer, their excitement growing. The sixth compass rose, as expected, was etched into the well's stone rim—but this time, it was different. Unlike the others, there was no directional bearing, no clue to follow. It was just the compass itself, a silent engraving staring back at them.

Sophie knelt by the edge, her excitement still vivid. "It's here," she breathed, leaning over the stone lip of the well, peering down into its dark depths. "This has to be it—the treasure must be at the bottom!"

But Claire hesitated, her practical mind refusing to accept the obvious. "Wait," she said, her voice cutting through the excitement. "It can't be."

Daniel and Sophie turned to her, confused. "What do you mean?" Sophie asked, her voice faltering slightly.

Claire rested her hand on the well's stonework, considering. "A well like this would have been crucial to the abbey. A main source of water. If Thomas or Edmund had hidden treasure down there, it would've been too risky. Wells were maintained, checked regularly. Someone would have found it."

Daniel's enthusiasm faltered as her words sank in. "You're right," he admitted. "Hiding treasure in a well—especially one so important to the abbey's function—would have been a huge risk."

Sophie's face fell, disappointment creeping into her expression. "Then why is the compass rose here?"

Claire crouched beside the well, studying the engraving. "It's still part of the clue. But this isn't the final destination. The well marks the end of this trail, but the treasure... it must be somewhere nearby."

The thrill of the hunt, momentarily dulled, surged back as they stood around the ancient well. They were close—closer than they'd ever been. The final piece of the puzzle was near, just waiting to be uncovered.

Chapter 23

5th November 1708 – Coast of England.

The night air hung heavy with mist as the rowboat glided silently through the water, its oars dipping rhythmically into the dark river. The *Endeavour* lay anchored offshore, her silhouette barely visible against the low-lying clouds. Edmund Grey, seated at the stern of the small boat, gazed back toward the bridge they had just left behind.

"Steady now," Edmund whispered, his voice barely audible over the soft lapping of water against the hull. Harper, the senior of his trusted men, nodded and began to stow the oars. Beside him, Briggs followed suit, his movements quiet and efficient. Both men had long ago earned Edmund's trust, but tonight's mission was of a different magnitude. If either spoke of what they had just done, it would mean the end of everything.

"Not a word," Edmund reminded his men, his voice firm but low.

Harper's eyes met his in the moonlight. "Aye, sir," he replied, his voice steady, with the same ironclad loyalty that had kept him alive through countless battles. Briggs simply nodded, his silence a mark of the trust that bound them.

The boat reached the side of the *Endeavour*, its hull dark and still as it rocked gently with the current. Edmund grabbed the rope ladder, pulling himself up the side of the ship with practised ease. Harper and Briggs followed without a sound, their boots landing softly on the deck as they rejoined the stillness of the night watch.

Above them, Captain Thomas Hastings stood in the shadows, waiting. His eyes flicked to Edmund as he stepped onto the deck, the unspoken question hanging between them.

"It's done," Edmund whispered, approaching Thomas with measured steps. "The treasure's hidden beneath the bridge. It'll stay there until we're ready to reclaim it."

Thomas nodded, his jaw set, tension etched in every line of his face. "Good. Tomorrow, we dock and hand over the Crown's share. They'll believe they've got it all. That's when we wait—bide our time until it's safe to act on the next step in our plan."

Edmund scanned the deck, ensuring no one was within earshot. The ship's night crew kept their distance, patrolling the ship in their usual disciplined silence. The crew were oblivious, believing that every chest and coin from their latest haul would be delivered to the Crown come morning.

As they spoke, Edmund's eyes flicked toward the faint glow on the horizon. He hesitated, then spoke, his voice low. "Thomas... it's Guy Fawkes Night. Those bonfires—how did we not account for this?"

Thomas's eyes widened slightly as the realization set in. "Damn," he muttered, running a hand through his hair. "How could we overlook something so obvious? Bonfires across the land, every soul awake and alert... We took a grave risk tonight, Edmund."

Edmund's voice held a note of tension. "I know. The irony isn't lost on me either. Here we are, hiding our own barrels beneath a bridge, just as Fawkes tried with his barrels of gunpowder." He paused, his voice barely a whisper. "It worries me, Thomas—what else might we have missed in our planning?"

"Once we dock," Thomas continued in a low tone, "we'll be under close watch. The Admiralty will inspect the cargo. We can't afford any mistakes. We give them exactly what they expect, nothing more."

Thomas drew in a breath, his gaze steady as he looked at Edmund. "We've both had our share of oversights, that's true. But Fawkes was betrayed; we've kept this plan between us and us only. We've not left ourselves open to the same fate." He placed a reassuring hand on Edmund's shoulder. "Listen, we've made it this far. The treasure is hidden, and the Admiralty is none the wiser. Trust in that."

"The men will fall in line," Edmund assured him, glancing back at Harper and Briggs, who had already blended into the shadows, invisible among the night watch. "They'll follow orders, same as always."

Thomas' gaze shifted toward the distant horizon, where the faint glow of Portsmouth flickered against the sky. "We have to ensure the treasure remains hidden for as long as it takes. One wrong move, and we lose it all."

Edmund understood the risks all too well. They had come this far—sailing through enemy-infested waters, battling storms and Spanish ships—and now, they stood on the precipice of either success or ruin. Every decision from here would be a test of their nerve, a delicate balance between deception and survival.

"We hand over the Crown's share," Edmund said, his voice resolute. "Then we wait. When the time is right. The treasure is safe. No one will find it."

Thomas gave a sharp nod, his face betraying none of the tension that coursed through him. "Good. Get some rest, Edmund. Tomorrow will test us all."

Edmund turned, his boots moving soundlessly across the deck. His mind, however, raced with the implications of their plan. The treasure, buried under that ancient bridge, felt like a tether pulling him toward an uncertain future. But he trusted Thomas. Together, they had survived battles, sieges, and betrayals. This would be no different.

As he descended below deck, he allowed himself a single moment of relief. The treasure was hidden. The next phase of the plan would unfold in the days to come. And, for now, no one could possibly suspect that a fortune lay buried just miles from Portsmouth, waiting to be reclaimed when the time was right.

Up on deck, Thomas stared out at the dark water, the seriousness of their scheme enveloping him like the cold night air. Tomorrow, they would face the Crown, and the game would begin in earnest. But tonight, they had bought themselves time. And in this deadly game of cat and mouse, time was everything.

Chapter 24

The late afternoon sun hung low over Titchfield Abbey, casting long, creeping shadows across the ancient stones. Daniel stood by the stone well, his gaze fixed on the sixth compass rose etched into its weathered surface. Unlike the previous ones, this compass offered no clear direction, no bearing. It was maddening—so close, yet the treasure remained frustratingly out of reach.

Sophie and Claire sat on the edge of the well, the two square letters spread between them. Their fingers traced the faded ink, their faces a mixture of concentration and frustration. They had deciphered so much already, yet something still eluded them.

Daniel's mind whirred as he watched them, dissecting the problem from every angle. Why no bearing? It didn't make sense. The previous compass roses had all been so precise, leading them step by step. But here, at the final piece of the puzzle, there was silence.

For a moment, Daniel looked out over the ruins of Titchfield Abbey, sensing the echoes of history surrounding him. The sun's golden rays stretched across the crumbling stone, and he couldn't shake the feeling of the moment's significance.

Sophie spoke up, a thoughtful crease forming between her brows. "It doesn't add up, Dad. Every other compass rose had a bearing... but this one? Nothing."

Claire chimed in, always the pragmatist. "Maybe Thomas wanted us to figure it out later. There must be more to it."

But Daniel wasn't satisfied with that. There had to be something else. His eyes drifted to the square letters again. He stared at them—perfectly symmetrical, identical in size. It seemed too deliberate. He was sure of it now. The shape of the parchment wasn't a coincidence.

"What if..." Daniel began, his voice almost a whisper, barely catching Sophie and Claire's attention. "What if the letters themselves are the compass?"

Sophie frowned, confused. "What do you mean?"

Daniel stepped forward, the idea taking shape in his mind. "Look at the letters. They're both square, and we've been so focused on the text. What if it's not just about what's written? What if they're meant to work together—physically?"

Claire's eyes narrowed with intrigue. "You mean, like... overlay them? Combine them somehow?"

"Exactly." Daniel nodded, feeling the pieces slot into place. "What if the letters themselves form a compass rose when we overlay them?"

Sophie handed him her letter, and Claire followed suit, a flicker of curiosity crossing her face. As Daniel held the two square parchments, he felt the essence of history in his hands. There was something important about them—he could sense it.

Daniel began with Edmund's letter, flipping it over. He'd noticed a faint "Z" on the back before, angled slightly, but hadn't given it much thought. Now, with a clearer idea forming in his mind, he turned the letter 45 degrees. As he did, the "Z" aligned perfectly to form an "N," marking true north.

"That's it," Daniel murmured, his pulse quickening. "Edmund marked north here."

He flipped Claire's letter over. The moment he did, a faint drawing caught his eye—a sketch of a ship. "The *Endeavour*," Daniel muttered, surprised. He hadn't seen the back of Claire's letter before. How had they missed this?

Claire glanced over, her eyes widening at the discovery. "I knew there was a drawing on the back, but I didn't think it was significant. I thought it was just a sketch of the *Endeavour*."

But it wasn't just the ship. Beneath the image were two words, barely visible under the worn surface: "50 chains."

Daniel's pulse quickened as the words registered. Fifty chains. It felt so specific, deliberate. His mind raced, wondering what it could mean.

As Daniel turned the letter, the ship rotated with it, the bow turning clockwise.

At first, nothing. The lines and markings on both letters seemed like random scrawls. But then, when the letter was turned exactly 45 degrees, the small, almost imperceptible markings on the edges of Claire's letter aligned perfectly with those on Edmund's. The symbols and lines fell into place within an instant. What had once seemed like scattered lines now formed a complete compass rose.

Sophie leaned in, her breath catching. "You did it."

Claire's eyes sparkled with excitement as she studied the newly revealed pattern. "It was there all along. Hidden in plain sight."

"It's pointing south," Daniel murmured, his voice tinged with awe. "The *Endeavour* is showing us the direction of the treasure."

The breeze shifted slightly, carrying the faint scent of damp stone and earth. In the distance, a lone bird called out, its cry echoing through the empty ruins. The stillness of the Abbey felt almost reverent, waiting for its secrets to be uncovered.

They stood in silence for a moment, taking in the revelation. Everything had been hidden within the letters—the compass rose, the ship, the direction of the treasure.

Daniel examined the drawing in more detail. "50 chains? What could that mean?" It was another clue, but its meaning wasn't immediately clear.

An undercurrent of anticipation hung over Titchfield Abbey, the sun dipping lower, casting golden hues across the landscape. As the compass rose etched into the letters pointed unmistakably south, a new clue had emerged—a set of faintly inscribed words beneath the image of the Endeavour on the back of Claire's letter: "50 chains."

Sophie squinted at the cryptic inscription. "Fifty chains? Could that be a reference to a harbour chain?" She glanced at Daniel, her voice uncertain but curious. "Remember the harbour chain we saw at The Round Tower? It stopped ships from entering the harbour, so maybe it's something similar."

Claire, equally baffled, looked between Sophie and Daniel. "It's possible, I guess. Ships, treasure... it could fit."

Daniel frowned, holding Claire's letter and examining the phrase with renewed focus. "It can't be an anchor or harbour chain," slowly turning the letter over and over in his hands. "A chain like that wouldn't give us a direction, let alone a precise measurement. There's something more here."

Sophie shrugged. "Maybe it's a metaphor, then? A symbol for something."

But Daniel's mind was already turning. The compass rose had given them a direction—south. Now, the Endeavour seemed to be pointing them towards the treasure. But "50 chains" felt too specific to be a simple metaphor. There had to be another meaning, a practical one.

"I don't think it's metaphorical or about an anchor chain," his tone growing more thoughtful. He glanced at the letters again, particularly at the compass rose etched into the parchment. "I think it's something else. Something to do with the distance."

Claire raised an eyebrow. "A distance? What makes you think that?"

Daniel gestured to the compass rose on the letters. "This symbol—this compass rose—has given us direction. South. But the '50 chains'... that sounds like a measurement to me. Chains... I've come across the term in old land surveys. It's a unit of length."

Sophie looked at him blankly. "Wait, *chains*? You mean like... an actual length?"

Daniel nodded. "Daniel nodded. 'Surveyors used chains to measure land, but I don't remember the exact length."

Claire leaned in, intrigued but still puzzled. "Surveyors? Like in old maps and land measurements?"

"Exactly," Daniel confirmed. "It's an old unit of measurement used for surveying land, but I don't know the precise conversion."

Sophie, ever the tech-savvy problem solver, pulled out her phone, fingers flying over the screen. "Let me check." She tapped through to a webpage and read aloud. "Here we go... A 'chain' refers to a unit of measurement equivalent to 66 feet, or roughly 20 meters."

Claire leaned over to peer at the screen. "So if it's 50 chains, how far is that?"

Sophie did a quick calculation, her face lighting up as she figured it out. "That's about 3,300 feet, or just over 1,000 metres. Around 0.7 miles."

Daniel's eyes gleamed with realisation. "That makes sense. Fifty chains south... that's the distance we need to travel."

Claire, now fully on board, glanced at the direction indicated by the compass rose. "So, we need to head 50 chains—about 0.7 miles—directly south from here."

Sophie nodded, confirming the distance with her app. "Looks like it."

Daniel smiled, the puzzle pieces clicking into place. "That's it. Thomas and Edmund must have used this old surveying method to mark the distance. They were naval men—they'd be familiar with this kind of precise measurement."

Sophie tapped quickly on her phone, pulling up the compass app and adjusting the settings. Her fingers moved with purpose as she locked the bearing. "I'll set it south," she muttered, her focus glued to the screen. "We can follow it from here."

Claire, always one step ahead, pulled out her phone, a confident smirk forming as she tapped the screen. "Or," she began, her tone laced with satisfaction, "we can let the drone do the work." Without missing a beat, she opened her drone app and programmed the coordinates with practiced precision. "I'll set it to follow the exact bearing and cover the distance. It'll lead us straight to the treasure."

Sophie raised an eyebrow, impressed, as she lowered her phone. "Looks like you've outsmarted me on this one. Let's see where it leads."

Daniel stood back, his gaze fixed on the drone as it whirred to life. As the drone rose into the sky, his heart pounded. Everything—the clues, the centuries-old letters—had led them here. Was the treasure really just fifty chains away? The excitement that had been mounting in his chest surged forward. The treasure, long hidden and shrouded in mystery, was finally within their grasp. They had cracked the code—the compass rose had given them direction, and the "50 chains" had revealed the distance.

As Claire's drone ascended into the sky, its path set to follow the course south, they all exchanged a look of shared anticipation. They were closer than ever now. The treasure was out there, waiting for them—just fifty chains away.

Chapter 25

6th November 1708 – Portsmouth Harbour.

As HMS *Endeavour* approached the narrow entrance to Portsmouth Harbour, Edmund Grey stood at the bow, his gaze fixed on the looming Round Tower. The ancient stone walls, worn by centuries of storms and battles, stood as a steadfast guardian over the harbour. After months at sea, navigating both natural dangers and enemy ships, Edmund allowed himself a quiet exhale. The sight of the tower symbolised safety and home—but beneath the surface, there was more.

Beside him, Captain Thomas Hastings remained silent, his sharp eyes scanning the harbour's defences and the bustling activity along the quay. Dockworkers moved with purpose, and naval officers kept their patrols, ensuring the harbour's security. Yet both Edmund and Thomas' thoughts lingered on the Round Tower, a powerful reminder of the Crown's ever-watchful eye. Portsmouth wasn't just a port—it was the heart of England's naval strength.

As the *Endeavour* sailed closer, a deep sense of awe spread among the crew. For Thomas and Edmund, the sight of the tower was more than just a symbol of homecoming; it represented the success of their mission and the dangerous secret they still carried.

Portsmouth Harbour had seen countless ships arrive and depart, each carrying the fate of the nation. Now, it welcomed the *Endeavour*, her weathered hull dark with the stains of salt and sea, bearing deep scars from cannon fire and storms alike. The rigging creaked as the ship glided forward, her sails tattered and patched from countless repairs. The deck was worn smooth underfoot, telling the silent story of months at sea, where every inch had been tested by wind, water, and warfare.

Thomas, hands steady on the wheel, guided the ship through the narrow passage, his eyes sharp, yet betraying the exhaustion that lingered from their long voyage. The masts of merchant ships and war vessels swayed gently in the breeze, their colours bright in contrast to the *Endeavour*'s battle-worn appearance. Dockworkers bustled along the quays, oblivious to the weight of the cargo aboard, while naval officers cast curious glances at the incoming ship. None could guess the true extent of what had been claimed on this perilous journey.

"Home, at last," Edmund muttered, his voice barely audible over the steady hum of the wind and sea. But he knew their journey was far from complete. The Crown's officials would demand an account of the treasure. What they didn't know was that only part of it had made its way to Portsmouth—the rest lay miles away, concealed beneath the arches of Stony Bridge.

As they neared the dock, Thomas turned to Edmund, his voice low. "We'll report to the Crown, hand over their share, and wait for the right moment to recover the rest."

Edmund nodded in agreement. There could be no mistakes. Each step from here had to be carefully executed. As the *Endeavour* slid into its berth, their secret seemed to press more urgently on his mind with each passing moment. Dockhands scrambled to tie the ship down while naval officers waited for the formalities to begin.

From the Round Tower, the Royal Navy's flag snapped in the breeze. Cannons boomed in salute, their echoes rolling across the harbour. The grand spectacle marked the ship's return, though few could comprehend the true value of its cargo. Edmund stood at the rail, watching the preparations with mounting tension.

His grip tightened on the wood as he surveyed the harbour. They had survived storms, battles, and betrayal, but now, back on home soil, the danger felt sharper. The treasure, disguised as ordinary cargo, was ready for inspection.

As the *Endeavour* came to a halt, excitement rippled through the crew. The prospect of dry land, fresh food, and pay was tantalisingly close. Yet whispers had already begun below deck, speculating on the true extent of the spoils. Unease lingered beneath the surface.

On the quay, senior naval officers, their uniforms pristine, waited for the ship to dock. Leading them was Admiral Sir George Patterson, a man whose reputation was as sharp as his sword. He had come to ensure the Crown received its due— every ounce of the spoils from the long and perilous voyage.

"Stow the sails!" Thomas commanded, his voice slicing through the flurry of activity. The crew obeyed at once, scaling the rigging with practiced precision. The sound of rustling canvas and the rhythmic creak of ropes filled the air as the sails were gathered and secured, leaving the ship ready for inspection.

As the ship settled, Thomas and Edmund exchanged a knowing glance. This was no routine homecoming. They stood at the gangway, offering crisp salutes as Patterson approached. The admiral's gaze swept across the deck with the practiced scrutiny of a man well-versed in naval operations.

"Captain Hastings. Lieutenant Grey," Patterson greeted, his tone formal. "The Crown is eager to see the fruits of your labour."

Thomas's expression darkened slightly as he spoke. "Before we proceed, sir, I must report the losses. Thirteen souls were claimed during the voyage—nine taken by battle, the others by sickness. The storm off the coast only worsened conditions." Patterson's jaw tightened, though he gave no other outward reaction. "A heavy cost," he muttered, his voice low but steady. "Their families will be notified at once."

Thomas nodded solemnly. "It was a hard journey, Admiral. But the men who survived have done their duty." He paused, glancing back toward the hold. "The treasure is ready for inspection, sir," he added more firmly.

Edmund remained still, his mind racing as the Crown's inspectors made their way toward the hold. The treasure aboard the ship was substantial, and the Crown's men would leave nothing unchecked.

As Patterson's men opened the chests and barrels, the gleam of gold and the shimmer of jewels caught in the dim light. One chest held stacks of gold coins, neatly arranged in rows, while another revealed silver ingots, each stamped with the seal of the Spanish crown. A third crate contained exquisite jewellery—necklaces, rings, and brooches adorned with precious gems that sparkled even in the gloom of the hold.

The wealth of their mission spilled out, piece by piece, each item carefully examined by the naval inspectors. One inspector ran his fingers over the edges of a gold coin, testing its weight, while another bent close to a string of pearls, inspecting the lustre. Murmurs of approval spread among the inspectors, their astonishment barely contained.

"An impressive haul," one of the inspectors muttered, clearly impressed. "The Crown will have much to celebrate."

Another inspector, eyeing the silver ingots, ran his hand over one of them. "There must be hundreds," he said quietly, the sound of metal ringing softly in the still air. "An exceptional quantity." Patterson nodded with satisfaction as the inventory grew. "The Crown will be pleased." His eyes gleamed with cold approval as his gaze settled on Thomas, lingering as if weighing something far beyond the treasure's worth. Edmund felt the tension coil tighter, but Thomas gave nothing away, his expression remaining unreadable.

Once the final chest had been counted and closed, Patterson's smile returned—thin and cold. "You've done England proud, Captain. Your success will not go unnoticed."

The lead inspector approached Patterson, ledger in hand. "The inventory is complete, sir. The volume of gold alone is enough to fund several naval campaigns."

Patterson gave a curt nod before turning back to Thomas and Edmund. "The Crown's expectations have been more than met. Prepare to offload the cargo. This will be taken directly to the treasury."

Thomas gave a respectful nod, the exchange formal but heavy. As the inspectors filed out, Edmund exhaled a quiet breath of relief. The first test had been passed. The Crown had its share. Now, they only needed to bide their time until they could recover the rest—the treasure still hidden beneath the Stony Bridge.

For the moment, their mission was complete. But as the sun began to set over Portsmouth Harbour, Edmund knew that the most dangerous part was still ahead.

Patterson's quartermaster approached next, each scratch of his quill seeming louder in the quiet. When he paused, tracing the list with narrowed eyes, Edmund's pulse quickened. The pressure seemed to close in on him, every second stretching painfully long.

Thomas stepped forward, his voice steady and authoritative. "The manifest is complete, sir. Every item has been thoroughly checked before docking. You'll find no discrepancies."

Patterson's cold gaze shifted from the manifest to Thomas. For a brief moment, the air seemed to hold its breath. Edmund could sense the intensity of the admiral's scrutiny, but Thomas remained still, unwavering under the pressure.

"Indeed." Patterson folded the manifest with deliberate precision, tucking it neatly under his arm. "Your crew has done well, Captain Hastings. A commendable journey, and a valuable haul for the Crown." He cast a brief glance at the barrels—his interest briefly stirred by the abundance of rum—but he dismissed it with a nod.

Edmund exhaled a silent breath as the tension dissipated. The officers turned to leave, and Thomas gave a subtle nod in Edmund's direction—an unspoken signal that the danger had passed, for now.

But the hidden fortune, the portion that would never appear on any manifest, remained far from Portsmouth Harbour. It would stay there, untouched and unseen, until the time came to recover it.

As the officers filed out of the hold, Edmund let out another quiet breath. They had passed this test. Their secret was still secure, but the pressure of it weighed heavily on both men.

The harbour was alive with activity as HMS *Endeavour* settled into its berth. Dockworkers in worn coats and flat caps moved with the efficiency of men well-versed in their trade, hoisting crates from vessels docked along the quay. The clatter of cargo and the creaking of wooden gangplanks filled the air. Ships of all sizes lined the docks, their masts reaching skyward against the dull grey clouds.

Thomas descended the gangplank first, his boots thudding against the cobblestones. Edmund followed closely, feeling the familiar sway beneath him dissipate with each step onto solid ground. His legs adjusted slowly, a lingering sense of the ship's motion adding a faint unsteadiness to his steps. The ground offered some relief, but the weight of the secret they carried clung to him, as inescapable as the rolling of the sea.

As they moved along the quay, lower-ranking sailors offered respectful nods and salutes. Thomas and Edmund carried themselves with the quiet authority of men who had seen and survived much. Despite the covert mission, their reputations preceded them, and they wore the confidence of seasoned naval officers.

"Captain Hastings! Lieutenant Grey!" A familiar voice called out from the bustling throng. They turned to see a tall figure weaving through the crowd—Commander John Hartley, an old comrade from their Mediterranean campaign. His face lit up with a broad grin as he approached, extending his hand.

"Still afloat, I see," Hartley chuckled, shaking Thomas' hand firmly before turning to Edmund. "Edmund, good to see you in one piece. I heard about the trouble with the Spanish off Cartagena."

Thomas offered a subtle smile. "Nothing we couldn't handle, Commander."

Edmund, his thoughts still preoccupied with the treasure, gave a more restrained greeting. "A few close calls, but the *Endeavour* held strong."

Hartley nodded knowingly, his expression one of respect and camaraderie. "You always manage to find your way through, don't you? The Crown's lucky to have men like you on the seas."

Before Thomas could respond, a call came from further down the quay—dockworkers beckoning for the next round of cargo to be unloaded. The constant activity of the port provided a perfect backdrop for Thomas and Edmund, allowing them to move unnoticed as their secret remained concealed.

"You'll have to excuse us, Commander." Thomas inclined his head in a polite gesture, his tone measured as he straightened his posture. "We've matters to address with the Admiralty."

Hartley smiled knowingly. "Of course. Duty calls. But do join me for a drink later—perhaps at *The Dolphin*? I'd love to hear more about the voyage."

"Perhaps," Thomas replied, his tone measured. "We'll see how the day unfolds."

As Hartley moved off, Thomas and Edmund continued through the bustling docks, nodding and returning salutes from sailors and dockworkers alike. Their quiet authority reassured those around them that everything was in order. But beneath the surface, Edmund knew that their true task was only just beginning.

The Admiralty office loomed ahead, its tall windows glinting in the afternoon light. Thomas cast a brief glance at Edmund, his voice low and firm. "No one knows what we've hidden. It must stay that way."

Edmund nodded, his resolve solidifying. "We've made it this far. We'll see it through."

With that, they walked onward, their faces calm, secrets well-guarded beneath the surface.

Chapter 26

The late afternoon sun hung low on the horizon, casting long shadows over the fields and countryside. The faint buzzing of Claire's drone hummed softly overhead, cutting through the stillness as they walked. Its camera feed was transmitted directly to Claire's phone, the image showing the path ahead as it hovered above, tracking their precise course southward—fifty chains, as indicated by the ancient letters.

Claire's eyes remained fixed on the live video stream. "We're nearly there." Her focus sharpened. "Just a few more chains to cover."

Daniel walked beside her, his gaze occasionally flickering to the phone screen, but his mind was focused on scanning the terrain around them, absorbing the shifting landscape. He could feel the intensity of their search increasing with each step—centuries of history converging on this moment. Sophie, however, was quieter than usual, holding her phone with the compass app open but remaining silent.

The path took them past a watermill pub, its old brick walls and ivy-covered windows standing in stark contrast to the modern cars parked out front. A cluster of locals gathered outside, laughter and chatter spilling into the quiet evening air. Sophie's eyes lingered on the building for a moment, as if grounding herself in something familiar before their journey took them further into the unknown.

"This is surreal," Sophie muttered, glancing from the compass on her phone to the mill, then back to the drone footage. "We've been chasing clues across cities, ancient landmarks… and now a quiet little village."

Daniel nodded but remained focused on the road ahead. "History is always hiding in plain sight."

They pressed on, crossing a busy road where cars rushed by, modernity a sharp contrast to the centuries-old trail they were following. The noise of traffic filled the air for a few moments, breaking the otherwise peaceful journey. As soon as they crossed the road, however, it felt like they had stepped into another time. The village of Titchfield opened before them, its narrow street lined with quaint stone houses, their Tudor timber frames and crooked chimneys adding a timeless charm.

Claire kept her eyes on the drone's feed as they walked down the quiet street. The drone led them further, nearing the old cemetery at the edge of the village. The path took them past crumbling stone walls, and soon, the trees that bordered the cemetery came into view.

"There's the cemetery," Claire murmured, her voice betraying a growing sense of excitement.

Sophie's unease returned, knotting her stomach. The ancient gravestones, some leaning with age, stood weathered and solemn, their surfaces eroded by time. She could almost sense the passage of centuries bearing down on them. She hesitated, glancing at Claire and then back at the drone hovering near the entrance.

As they crossed the threshold into the cemetery, Sophie spoke softly, her voice barely above a whisper, "Are you guys thinking what I'm thinking?"

Daniel nodded solemnly, his eyes sweeping across the rows of headstones, overgrown grass, and moss-covered stone markers. "The treasure... it might be buried here. In a grave."

Sophie stiffened, her discomfort turning to dread. "I don't like this, Dad. We're not grave robbers. This feels wrong."

Claire, ever pragmatic, shrugged. "We're not disturbing anything. We can at least check the headstones, see if anything stands out—something connected to Edmund or Thomas."

Sophie remained uneasy, glancing at the weathered stones, but Claire's point was fair. "Let's just be careful," Sophie muttered. "If we're wrong, I don't want to cause any damage."

As they ventured deeper into the cemetery, following the drone's soft hum, Claire found her gaze drifting to Sophie, noticing the discomfort etched on her face. Surprisingly, a feeling of sympathy began to well up. She hadn't thought much of Sophie beyond her role in this treasure hunt, but now, watching her unease, Claire's perception shifted. If she'd ever had a daughter, she realised, she'd want her to have qualities like Sophie's—thoughtful, cautious, and grounded.

Another thought struck her: Sophie's grandfather, Daniel's father, had recently passed away. Standing here among the gravestones, she understood that this place might carry a different weight for them. This wasn't just about history—it was something more personal.

The final piece of the puzzle felt tantalisingly close, yet the air around them seemed to grow heavier, carrying the weight of their own past and the secrets they were unearthing. The echoes of history surrounded them, as if the centuries-old mystery they were chasing had joined them in the cemetery, observing their every move in silence.

Sophie's footsteps slowed as she scanned the rows of ancient headstones, the eerie quiet of the cemetery pressing in around her. She had been trailing behind Claire and Daniel, her mind preoccupied with the unsettling thought of searching for treasure among the dead. But then, something caught her eye. She froze, her breath hitching slightly.

"Guys... come look at this."

Her voice cut through the silence, drawing Claire and Daniel's attention. They turned, seeing her standing near the far wall of the cemetery, her eyes fixed on a particular gravestone. With a shared sense of urgency, they hurried over to where she stood.

The headstone before them was weathered by centuries, its once-clear markings now softened by time. But even in its age, the name etched into the stone was unmistakable: *Grey Hastings*. Below the name, a simple yet poignant message: *A Son, A Father*.

Claire was the first to speak, her tone laced with disbelief. "Grey Hastings... It's their names, combined. Hastings and Grey."

Daniel knelt before the gravestone, his fingers gliding over the worn letters. His heart raced as the significance of history and the reality of their discovery washed over him in a rush. But it was what lay beneath the name that truly captured their attention.

At the base of the stone, partially hidden by moss and dirt, was the faint carving of a Tudor rose. But upon closer inspection, Daniel's eyes widened. Within the intricate petals of the rose was something more—a compass rose, subtly embedded in the design.

Daniel's mind raced as he examined the carving more closely. It was all there—the Tudor rose, the compass rose, and the names that tied everything together. Grey Hastings. Their ancestors had left a clue, a marker of their legacy, hidden in plain sight.

But then, something else caught Daniel's eye—something almost too perfect to be accidental. At the very centre of the compass rose, faintly etched, was an "X."

His breath caught as he pointed it out to Claire and Sophie. "Look. Right here. X marks the spot."

Claire blinked, staring at the faint mark. "You've got to be kidding."

Daniel stepped closer, his breath catching as realization dawned. "No." His words trembled with a mixture of excitement and awe. "It makes sense. They hid the treasure beneath this grave, beneath the marker of their own names, and left the compass rose... and the 'X' to show us exactly where."

The realisation hung heavy in the air, the centuries-old mystery finally unravelled before them.

The reality of their discovery loomed over the trio as they stood by the gravestone. The air around them felt dense, and Sophie's earlier excitement quickly shifted to unease. Her gaze lingered on the weathered stone, her heart racing for an entirely different reason now. The thrill of the hunt had faded, replaced by a moral conflict she hadn't anticipated.

Sophie's voice trembled as she broke the silence, her eyes filled with uncertainty. "We can't disturb someone's grave... It's not right."

Her words hung in the air, casting a long shadow over their recent breakthrough. Claire folded her arms, her gaze softening as she noticed the hesitation in Sophie's expression. She'd expected resistance, but she also understood the weight this place might carry for Sophie.

"Sophie," Claire began, her tone steady but thoughtful, "I know this isn't easy. But this grave isn't just any spot—it's a marker left by Thomas and Edmund, intended for us. They didn't bury the treasure randomly; they buried it for their families to find, when the time was right. We're not disturbing anything. If anything, we're honouring their wishes."

Sophie swallowed hard, her throat tight with emotion. She wanted to believe Claire, to trust that this was just part of the treasure hunt, but something deep inside resisted. "But it's still a grave. People—families—are buried here. There's something sacred about that."

Daniel stood a few steps away, his hand resting on the gravestone. His face was a mask of quiet contemplation, caught between his historian's reverence for the past and the practical realities of the situation. He had always approached his research with respect, careful to tread lightly around the lives and legacies of those who had come before. Now, the lines were blurred. His own ancestor's hand had drawn him here, and yet...

Claire's voice softened as she looked at Sophie. "Do you really think they would have gone through all this trouble—leaving us letters, creating this trail—if they didn't want their families to uncover it? Thomas and Edmund knew this would be found one day. They trusted us to finish what they started."

Sophie's heart ached with the conflict, her mind racing between duty to the past and loyalty to the present. She glanced at her father, seeking an anchor in his quiet resolve.

Daniel let out a slow breath, his voice low but steady. "It's a difficult line, Sophie. But Claire has a point. If this is where they hid the treasure… they didn't want it to be lost forever." He paused, the seriousness of the decision weighing on him. "But we need to be sure. This can't be something we take lightly."

Sophie's eyes filled with unshed tears. "I just don't know if I can do this… Not like this."

The trio stood in heavy silence, the gravestone of Grey Hastings at their feet, and the treasure of their ancestors buried somewhere beneath. The past and present were colliding, and the choice before them was more than just about treasure—it was about legacy, about honour, about family.

The gravestone of Grey Hastings rose before them, a stark reminder of the past, as Sophie's inner turmoil intensified. Silence enveloped the group, but Daniel's thoughts were anything but quiet. He rested a hand on the stone, his mind swirling with questions he hadn't anticipated.

He found himself imagining Edmund and Thomas in those final moments—two men driven by duty, honour, and desperation. This treasure had remained buried because they didn't make it back. It had never been part of their original plan. They had trusted that they would return, retrieve it themselves, but fate had intervened. They had never come home.

His thoughts drifted further, conjuring up images of that night. What were they thinking as they buried the treasure? Had they performed a makeshift ceremony, offering a prayer for protection over their hidden trove? Or was it done in haste, hands trembling with the knowledge that they were leaving behind something of immense value? Daniel could almost see them in the dead of night, looking over their shoulders, praying they weren't seen, knowing they might never set foot on this soil again.

He swallowed hard, his throat dry. If Edmund and Thomas had lived, they would have returned in secret to retrieve it. But if they had been caught... *would they have been branded as thieves?*

Daniel's gaze turned distant as he considered the implications. If they uncovered the treasure now, centuries later... *Would they, too, be considered accomplices in a crime?* The treasure had originally belonged to the Crown, and Edmund and Thomas had concealed a portion of it. Uncovering it might bring accusations of theft, even now. The legal implications were murky at best. As a historian, Daniel had always followed the rules of preservation and respect. But this was different. This was personal.

His heart raced as the questions piled up. *Was this what his father had realized all along? Had he known the risks and chosen to leave it in the past, where it belonged?* Daniel hadn't seen it that way before, but now... it seemed almost as if his father had been protecting them, sparing them from the echoes of secrets. How had he not thought of this sooner?

He glanced at Sophie, her features taut with the same uncertainty. It wasn't just about disturbing a grave; it was about the implications of their actions, the consequences of unearthing something that had been hidden for so long. The Crown's reach extended across the centuries—if they took this treasure, would they find themselves caught in its grasp?

His pulse quickened, the enormity of the situation finally hitting him. He had always known this journey would come with risks, but now, standing here, staring at the gravestone of his ancestor, the reality was sinking in.

Edmund and Thomas had buried a secret. And now, so many years later, it was Daniel, Sophie, and Claire who would have to decide whether to dig it back up.

His mind continued to race, spiralling with possibilities and consequences. Had Edmund and Thomas feared the same thing? Did they worry that their families would face punishment for retrieving what had been stashed away? Did they bury the treasure knowing full well it might never see the light of day again? He ran a hand over his face. "So many questions...", barely audible to Sophie and Claire. "I didn't realise how many answers we'd need before we could even think about moving forward."

Sophie looked up at her father, catching the quiet turmoil in his voice. "What do we do, Dad?" Her voice was soft, filled with the same mix of fear and uncertainty he was feeling.

Daniel inhaled slowly, steadying himself. "I don't know yet." He looked between Sophie and Claire, his eyes filled with conflicting emotions. "But whatever we do... we need to be sure."

For the first time since their journey began, Daniel wasn't sure what the right course of action was. They were on the precipice of something extraordinary, but stepping over that line might come with consequences none of them were prepared for.

Chapter 27

8th May 1709 – Mediterranean Sea.

Dawn was breaking, casting a soft, golden glow across the calm sea. The *Endeavour* creaked gently as it cut through the water, its sails full and billowing. The sky above was streaked with the first hints of light, but the horizon ahead remained dark, heavy with the promise of what was to come. The Spanish fleet, still distant, loomed like a shadow on the edge of their vision.

Lieutenant Edmund Grey stood by the railing, his hands gripping the weathered wood as he gazed out over the vast expanse of water. The sea, so deceptively tranquil, seemed to mock the storm brewing within him. Beside him, Captain Thomas Hastings stood tall, his expression composed, yet the significance of the moment was etched deeply into his features.

There was a silence between them, but it was the kind shared by men who had faced death together many times before. They didn't need to speak to understand what was at stake. This wasn't just another battle—it was their final stand, one way or another. The treasure they had hidden in England, their shared secret, hung heavy in the air between them.

Edmund broke the silence first, his voice low and almost a whisper, as if saying the words would make them true. "If we don't make it through this..." He paused, the impact of his words sinking in. "The letters will be our legacy."

Thomas, ever the pragmatist, turned slightly, his gaze still fixed on the horizon. His face was calm, but there was a hardness to his eyes, a steeliness that had carried him through countless battles. "The letters are our safeguard," he said, his voice steady. "If we don't make it back, our families will follow the clues and secure what we've hidden. It's how we'll protect our legacy—for generations to come."

Edmund nodded, a sense of unease settling deep within him. The letters—those small, fragile pieces of parchment—held everything they had worked for. They were the key to the treasure they had hidden away, a legacy meant for their families. If they failed today, if the sea claimed them, the letters would be all that remained.

The horizon shifted, the dark shapes of the Spanish ships becoming clearer, more defined against the lightening sky. Edmund's pulse quickened, the familiar rush of battle nerves stirring in his veins, but beneath it all was the knowledge that this fight wasn't just about survival. It was about ensuring the treasure they had hidden, the secret they had guarded so closely, remained untouched by the Crown.

Thomas exhaled slowly, the sound barely audible above the creak of the ship. "We knew this was coming," he said, more to himself than to Edmund. "We've always known."

Edmund's gaze dropped to the deck, his mind drifting back to the night they had buried the treasure. He recalled the heaviness of the burden and the cold river water lapping at their boots as they concealed it beneath rocks and mud, deep under the bridge. They had worked in silence, the significance of the task pressing upon them, fully aware that if they never returned, the treasure could remain there, lost forever.

"It's strange," Edmund murmured, his voice heavy with unspoken emotion. "To think that everything we've done might end here, in this sea."

Thomas turned to him then, his eyes locking onto Edmund's. "Not everything." His tone was firm, resolute. "We've done our part. The treasure is safe. The letters will guide them, if not us."

Edmund nodded, though the words did little to settle the uneasy feeling in his stomach. The Spanish fleet was closing in, the calm sea beneath them a stark contrast to the chaos that was about to erupt. His fingers tightened around the railing as a dull, hazy light filtered through the clouds, barely illuminating the deck.

The Spanish ships loomed on the horizon, their dark sails cutting through the mist as they approached with ominous intent. A sense of unease settled over the scene, but Thomas, ever unshaken, broke the silence with a grin.

"You ever hear the one about the pirate who walked into a tavern with a ship's wheel attached to his trousers?" he asked, glancing at Edmund.

Edmund raised an eyebrow, managing a half-smile despite the tension. "No, what happened?"

Thomas chuckled, watching the ships draw closer. "Tapster says, 'Why've you got a ship's wheel on your trousers?' Pirate replies, 'Arrr, it's turning me nuts.'"

Edmund laughed, shaking his head as he turned back to the approaching fleet. "God help us if you try that on the crew."

A strong gust whipped past them, carrying with it the hollow creak of the ship's rigging and the distant shouts of the crew preparing for battle. The rhythmic slap of the waves against the hull echoed in Edmund's ears, a steady reminder of the ocean's pull. He clenched his fists, feeling the rough texture of the worn wood beneath his fingers as he braced himself for what was to come.

Thomas straightened, his voice carrying a quiet finality. "We're ready. Whatever happens today, we've done all we can."

Edmund nodded, the unspoken words lingering between them. They had fought countless battles together, but this one felt different. There was a weight to it, a sense that this was the end of their journey. The letters, the treasure, the legacy they had built—it all came down to this.

As the Spanish ships loomed closer, their flags snapping in the wind, Edmund squared his shoulders, his heart pounding in his chest. The calm before the storm was over.

Below decks, the cramped, shadowed quarters of *HMS Endeavour* were alive with the sounds of war preparation. The metallic ring of swords being sharpened, the dull thud of cannonballs rolling into position, and the barked orders of officers echoed through the ship. Lanterns swayed with the rhythm of the sea, casting flickering light on the crew as they scrambled to make ready for the coming storm.

Captain Thomas Hastings moved among them with authority, his voice carrying above the din. "Prepare the starboard guns! Keep the powder dry!" His commands were sharp, his presence a steady anchor amid the chaos. The crew, seasoned from countless battles, responded with precision, their movements efficient and practised. But beneath their disciplined calm, there was an undercurrent of tension. They all knew what lay ahead.

Lieutenant Edmund Grey moved through the gun deck, his steps slow and deliberate, the sounds of battle preparations around him fading into a distant murmur. His mind was preoccupied—not with the impending conflict but with the secret he and Thomas bore. The grave in the quiet churchyard of Titchfield, marked by a headstone bearing their names, lingered in his thoughts.

As his fingers traced the smooth, worn wood of a cannon, the memory of the night they buried the treasure came flooding back. It wasn't a hasty or covert operation, as one might expect. No, it had been an official, solemn affair. Under the watchful eyes of a local vicar, they had stood there in the moonlight, Thomas beside him, two grave diggers and the vicar bearing witness to what appeared to be a respectful burial.

The headstone, carved with the names *Grey Hastings* and the inscription, *A Son, A Father,* had been placed there by the stoneworkers earlier that day. The vicar had spoken a few quiet words, unaware of the real nature of the burial he was blessing.

Only Edmund, Thomas, and that silent grave beneath the churchyard knew the truth—the treasure, wrapped in secrecy, was now nestled in the ground, disguised as a memorial. It was the perfect ruse. If they returned victorious, the treasure would remain there, awaiting the right moment to be retrieved. If not, the letters they had carefully crafted would guide their descendants to the riches buried beneath that sacred earth.

Edmund's gaze wandered across the deck, settling on Thomas, who was issuing his final orders with the same calm, composed manner he always carried. The captain caught

Edmund's eye, and for a fleeting moment, they exchanged a silent understanding.

It had all seemed so clear in the planning—the treasure, the letters, the pact they had made. But now, as the enormity of their secret pressed down on Edmund, it felt almost suffocating. The grave was official, the treasure buried beneath the feet of the faithful, marked by a headstone that would mislead anyone who glanced at it.

Would it remain hidden if they didn't return? The question tormented at him. Would their families even know to find it?

Thomas' words echoed in his mind: "The Crown doesn't need to know everything." But now, with the Spanish fleet bearing down on them, their ships' outlines growing sharper against the horizon, the burden of what they had done felt heavier than ever.

They had buried more than treasure that night; they had buried their hopes and fears, their futures, all beneath the earth.

His hand tightened on the cannon's side as the memory washed over him. *All this—was it worth it?* The thought crept into his mind unbidden, a whisper in the midst of the noise around him.

"All this... was it worth it?" he murmured quietly, almost to himself, the question hanging heavy in the air.

Unbeknownst to him, Thomas had approached from behind. The captain's sharp eyes softened as he overheard Edmund's words. A sad, knowing smile crossed his lips. "It was worth the risk, " Thomas replied quietly, his voice cutting through the noise but carrying an unexpected warmth. "If we succeed, we protect our families. If not..." He glanced towards the deck above where the cannons were being loaded, the thud of boots overhead signalling the preparations. "The treasure will."

Edmund turned to face his old friend, the depth of their secret evident in both their eyes. For a brief moment, the battle ahead felt distant, almost surreal. What mattered most now was what they had left behind—the treasure, the letters, the legacy that could outlast them.

"The Crown doesn't need to know everything," Thomas added in a lower voice, stepping closer. His gaze was steady, resolute, though Edmund could sense the same uncertainty lingering beneath his calm exterior. "We made a pact. We follow through, and if we fall... well, then the Crown gets what it thinks is all of the spoils."

Edmund managed a faint smile, a sense of relief washing over him at Thomas' pragmatism. "The letters... they'll guide them, won't they?"

Thomas nodded firmly. "They will. We've left enough clues. But for now, we focus on survival."

The ship rocked gently beneath their feet as they stood in shared silence, their pact sealed not by words but by the unspoken understanding between them. The sounds of battle preparation rumbled around them, but in that moment, it was as if time had slowed. Edmund's mind flickered back to the letters, the delicate parchment folded carefully, hidden in their private quarters. If they didn't make it through today, those letters would be all that remained of their mission.

With a final glance exchanged between them, Thomas clapped a firm hand on Edmund's shoulder. "Come, Lieutenant. The sea waits for no man."

Edmund nodded, squaring his shoulders. The battle was coming, and the time for doubt had passed. Together, they strode towards the deck, ready to face the storm.

The deck of HMS *Endeavour* groaned under the strain, wood creaking as the ship cut through the Mediterranean waters. The air hung heavy with tension, every man bracing for what was about to unfold. The Spanish ships were now bearing down, their sails fully unfurled and the details of their cannons visible, ready to strike. Each ship, closing fast, bore down on them with deadly intent.

The sharp crack of cannon fire shattered the stillness. Smoke billowed from the gun ports as the first volley was unleashed. The *Endeavour* shook violently, its hull reverberating with the thunder of battle. Cannonballs whistled overhead, splintering wood as they struck, sending shards flying through the air.

"Hold steady!" Captain Thomas Hastings barked, his voice cutting through the chaos. He stood firm at the helm, his hand gripping the rail with a white-knuckled grip. His eyes were locked on the approaching Spanish galleons, calculating every move, every breath. "Bring us to port! Ready the starboard cannons!"

Lieutenant Edmund Grey was by his side, his expression grim, yet his movements remained steady. He was no stranger to battle, but this one felt different—more burdensome. The thought of their hidden treasure nagged at the back of his mind. It wasn't just the Spanish they fought; it was fate itself.

Edmund's eyes darted across the deck as the crew scrambled to their positions. Sailors, drenched in sweat and powder, manned the guns, their faces hardened by years of naval warfare. Shouts filled the air, mingling with the deafening blasts of cannon fire. The sea churned around them, foaming and blackened by smoke.

"Fire!" Thomas roared, his voice carried by the wind. The *Endeavour* unleashed another broadside, the recoil jolting the ship as a hail of iron shot tore through the advancing Spanish line. For a moment, hope flickered. They were holding their ground.

"Reload! Faster, damn it!" Edmund urged the crew, moving between them, helping to direct the fire. A surge of urgency coursed through him, not from fear but from the knowledge that this could be their last stand. His gaze met Thomas' for a brief second—two men bound by a pact, both fully aware of the stakes.

The battle surged on, each exchange more violent than the last. The Spanish fleet was relentless, their galleons closing in, their cannons returning fire with deadly precision. The *Endeavour* shuddered as another salvo struck its hull, sending tremors through the deck.

"She can take it!" Thomas yelled, his voice defiant against the storm of cannon fire. "Keep firing!"

But the tide was turning. More Spanish ships had joined the fray, surrounding the *Endeavour*. The odds were shifting, the threat of the enemy pressing in on them like a vice.

Edmund could feel the momentum slipping. The deck beneath him lurched violently as another cannonball slammed into the side of the ship, ripping through the lower decks. Smoke and flame curled up from below, the acrid smell of burning wood stinging his eyes.

"Brace!" Thomas called, as the Spanish unleashed a brutal barrage.

The ship shook violently, and Edmund was thrown against the rail, clutching it to steady himself. Blood and sweat mingled on the deck as the crew fought on, but Edmund knew—deep down—that they were losing. The Spanish fleet was closing in from all sides, cannons roaring, as the *Endeavour* was torn apart.

Thomas met Edmund's gaze again, and this time, there was no need for words. They both knew how this would end. There was a silent acceptance between them, a recognition of the inevitable. Yet, they fought on, determined to make the Spanish pay dearly for their victory.

Another explosion rocked the deck, and Thomas staggered. His hand instinctively went to his side, where a shard of splintered wood had pierced him. Blood seeped through his uniform, but he remained upright, his face pale but resolute.

Edmund rushed to his side, his voice low but urgent. "Thomas, you're hit."

Thomas gritted his teeth, shaking his head. "It doesn't matter. Keep fighting, Edmund. Don't let them—" His words were cut off as another cannon blast roared through the air, striking the ship with brutal force.

Edmund looked around at the carnage—the broken bodies of the crew, the flames licking at the deck, the Spanish galleons circling like vultures. The *Endeavour* was sinking, the sea creeping up its sides, pulling it down into the abyss.

Edmund's mind raced as the water surged around his feet. He thought of the treasure buried beneath the earth, hidden beneath the gravestone they had so carefully marked. Thomas' words echoed in his mind: *The letters are our legacy.*

He cast one last glance at Thomas, who was slumped against the rail, bloodied but defiant. And then, with the roar of the sea filling his ears, Edmund knew their time had run out.

The battle was lost.

The *Endeavour* was crumbling around him, her hull shattered by cannon fire. Smoke and flames swirled across the deck, and the cries of wounded men echoed in the chaos. Lieutenant Edmund Grey, bloodied and battered, stood at the heart of the destruction, gripping the hilt of his sword tightly. The ship groaned under the force of the Spanish onslaught, but Edmund's resolve remained unshaken.

All around him, chaos reigned. The *Endeavour*—once their hope, their pride—was sinking fast, battered by the relentless fire of the Spanish fleet. The sea surged angrily against its sides, swallowing the debris as the ship slowly descended into its watery grave. Spanish soldiers were already boarding, climbing over the ruined hull, weapons drawn.

Edmund's gaze flickered to the lifeless form of Captain Hastings, crumpled against the mainmast, his chest stained with blood from the fatal wound that had ended his life. His closest friend and comrade was gone, but Edmund knew Thomas had died with the same sense of duty that had driven them both—an unwavering commitment to protecting their families and ensuring the Crown's treasure was kept safe.

Grief and rage surged within him, but it wasn't directed at the Crown. No, their duty had always been clear. It was the enemy before him—the Spanish—who sought to take everything they had fought for. They would not succeed.

Edmund fought with a grim determination, swinging his sword against the advancing Spanish soldiers. His movements were precise, fuelled not by desperation but by a steadfast resolve. He knew, even in these final moments, that the letters—those fragile pieces of parchment—held everything. The future, the legacy of both his and Thomas' families, was hidden in a graveyard back in England, guarded by nothing more than a simple headstone. And no one, not the Spanish, not the Crown, would ever know the full truth.

As the ship sank lower into the sea, Edmund could feel the deck tilting beneath his feet. The relentless waves were rising higher, licking at his boots as the *Endeavour* began to vanish beneath the surface. He exchanged one last, defiant look at the Spanish soldiers closing in on him, then turned to face the sea.

Thomas' words lingered in his mind, a vow etched in both their hearts: "If we fall, the treasure will remain hidden, waiting for those destined to find it."

The *Endeavour* lurched again, and Edmund was violently thrown into the sea. The cold water struck him like a hammer, stealing the breath from his lungs. He struggled to stay afloat, but the heaviness of his uniform and his injuries dragged him down. The waves surged over his head, and the roar of battle faded into a muffled cacophony as the sea engulfed him.

For a moment, in the cold, murky depths, Edmund's thoughts drifted to the letters, the treasure, and the families he had sworn to protect. Even as the sea claimed him, he felt a strange sense of peace. The secret would die with him, but the legacy would live on.

This treasure will never belong to the Crown... or to the enemy, Edmund thought, his last conscious breath slipping away as the darkness closed in around him.

And then, silence.

The waters of the Mediterranean calmed once more as the Spanish fleet sailed away, victorious. Debris from the *Endeavour* floated on the surface, the proud ship now resting at the bottom of the sea. The battle was over, but the Spanish, in their triumph, remained unaware of what they had truly left behind.

The crew of the *Endeavour* had fought valiantly, but the cost had been high. Thomas and Edmund were lost, their bodies claimed by the sea. They had perished as heroes, burdened by their mission and the secret they had taken to their graves. Their treasure remained hidden, safely buried far from the turmoil of battle, out of reach of the Spanish victors.

As the waves lapped gently at the wreckage, the legacy of Thomas and Edmund endured. Their letters, and the treasure they guarded, would survive them, waiting to be discovered by those who knew where to look. For now, the sea kept its silence, and the *Endeavour* lay in her watery grave, a forgotten casualty of war.

But the story of Thomas and Edmund was not over. Their secret would live on, waiting for the day when it would be revealed.

Chapter 28

Daniel, Sophie, and Claire stood by the edge of the dig, waiting. The graveyard was still, with only the low thud of shovels hitting the damp earth breaking the silence. Bright midday sunlight cast clear shadows across the scene, illuminating every detail.

A team of archaeologists, hands steady but hearts racing, worked diligently to unearth the casket that had been concealed beneath the gravestone of Grey Hastings for over three centuries. The importance of history and the promise of unimaginable wealth hung in the air around them.

Daniel stood slightly apart, eyes fixed on the headstone marked with the words, "A Son, A Father." He could barely comprehend that beneath that stone lay the answer to a mystery that had eluded his family for generations.

Why didn't my father pursue this? The question still lingered in Daniel's mind, growing more insistent as they got closer to the treasure. His father had known about the legend, about the letters and the clues passed down, but he had never chased them. He'd called it a fool's errand, dismissing it as something better left to history. *Maybe he didn't want to dig up old wounds. Or maybe... he wasn't ready to confront the past.* It was something Daniel had never fully understood until now, standing here on the brink of revelation. History had a grip stronger than he'd expected. His father had chosen not to bear it—Daniel wondered if he should have done the same.

"It's hard to believe," Sophie murmured, standing beside him, her eyes wide with awe. "After everything, it's here. Just beneath the surface."

Daniel nodded slowly. "If Thomas and Edmund had survived, we wouldn't be standing here. This treasure would have been collected long ago, divided among their families."

As the casket was slowly raised from the ground, the wooden exterior, though worn and weathered, had miraculously withstood the test of time. It was unlike any ordinary casket, heavier, reinforced to conceal the treasure buried within.

One of the lead archaeologists wiped his brow and glanced over at Daniel, his voice tinged with excitement. "This is it. It's been undisturbed all these years. We'll open it once we've ensured the condition is stable."

Daniel, Sophie, and Claire exchanged glances. The thrill of discovery was tempered by the significance of what lay inside— the fortune, the legacy, and the consequences.

While the archaeologists worked, an official from the Crown approached, a clipboard in hand, his expression professional yet curious. He glanced at the trio, knowing full well the magnitude of what was about to be revealed.

"Just so we're all clear," the official began, flipping through documents, "the Crown's portion of the original treasure was worth £538,875 in 1708. In today's terms, that's approximately £124 million."

Sophie's eyes widened. "That much?"

Daniel, though a historian and used to large figures, felt his heart race. "The Crown received all of that from Thomas and Edmund's mission?"

"Indeed," the official confirmed. "What was declared and handed over was an extraordinary amount of gold and silver, along with various artifacts. But the Crown, of course, didn't know there was more."

Claire raised an eyebrow. "And the treasure here, the one buried in this grave?"

The official paused for a moment, as if calculating. "If what we estimate is correct, we're looking at around 150 kilograms of gold and jewels, hidden away by Thomas and Edmund for their families. Today, based on the price of gold alone, we're talking about a figure around £10 to £12 million. But with the historical value of the jewels and artifacts, that number could rise significantly."

Daniel's mind whirled as he tried to process the numbers. This wasn't just a personal discovery anymore—it was a historical revelation that could change how his family, and perhaps the world, viewed the events of 1709.

Would my father have understood this moment if he were here? The thought tugged at Daniel. His father had never believed it would come to this—the letters, the clues, the chase for treasure. He had dismissed it all as legend, as something better left untouched. But Daniel had pushed forward, believing in the legacy. And now, standing on the cusp of uncovering the truth, he couldn't help but wonder if he had done the right thing. *Was it just treasure we were after, or something deeper?* The legacy his father had avoided was now Daniel's to claim—or to let go.

With a final nod from the archaeologists, the casket was placed on solid ground. Daniel stepped forward, his hands trembling slightly as he reached for the latch. Claire and Sophie stood on either side of him, each one holding their breath, their unease filling the silence.

The casket creaked as it opened, revealing its contents beneath a layer of protective cloth. The air seemed to still as the cloth was pulled back to reveal the glint of gold and the unmistakable gleam of precious jewels, nestled among the relics of a long-forgotten age.

Jewels, rings, and coins were piled neatly within the casket, sparkling in the bright midday light. The treasure was real—more real than they had ever dared to imagine. The wealth that had been hidden for centuries now lay exposed before them.

Sophie gasped. "It's... incredible."

Claire's eyes remained fixed on the treasure, but the rush of excitement that had driven her for so long began to fade. The gold, the jewels—they were there, just as she had imagined. Yet as she stood in front of the gleaming pile, she felt a weight lift in an unexpected way. This wasn't just a fortune—it was her ancestor's legacy. *Thomas Hastings.* He had risked everything for this, hidden it for their family. And now, she had brought that story to its conclusion. But at what cost?

She had sacrificed so much—time, relationships, parts of her life she might never get back. For a moment, doubt clouded her mind. *Was it really worth it?* But then, her gaze drifted to Daniel and Sophie. She watched the way they shared this moment—the awe in their eyes, the way they stood together, united in something far deeper than treasure.

Maybe that's the real reward, Claire thought, feeling a sense of peace she hadn't expected. She had chased history, but along the way, she had witnessed something beautiful—Daniel and Sophie, father and daughter, rediscovering their connection through this journey. And in that, she saw something worth all the sacrifices. Maybe it wasn't about the gold after all.

Daniel's voice was barely above a whisper, his eyes locked on the casket's contents. "This is what they died for. Thomas an Edmund."

Claire, pragmatic as always, glanced between the treasure and Daniel. "And now, it's up to us what happens next."

The official approached, eyeing the contents with professional detachment, though his voice betrayed his awe. "The Crown will want to assess the historical significance of each piece before making any formal declarations."

But Daniel was barely listening, his mind fixed on the past—the sacrifices made, the lives lost, and the treasure they had sworn to protect. It was more than just gold. It was a legacy, buried for over three hundred years, finally unearthed.

As the last rays of sunlight disappeared behind the horizon, the three stood together, their long search coming to a climactic end. The treasure gleamed before them, a testament to history, but in the stillness that followed, a new kind of tension settled over the group—a quieter, more personal one.

Sophie was the first to break the silence, her fingers tapping on her phone as she pulled up a local map. "Right," she said, glancing between them with a sly grin. "There's a cafe just around the corner. Anyone fancy a cream tea?"

Claire didn't miss a beat. "Only if it's cream before jam," she replied with mock seriousness.

Daniel turned to them, raising an eyebrow as a soft smile flickered at the corner of his mouth. "First time for everything." He let out a sigh, shaking his head.

They shared a quick laugh, the heaviness of history momentarily lifting as they set off into the early afternoon, leaving the treasure and the graveyard behind, but not forgotten.

Glossary and Historical Notes

Portsmouth Harbour

A significant harbour on the southern coast of England, Portsmouth Harbour has served as a key naval base for centuries. The harbour's strategic location made it an ideal site for shipbuilding and defence, and it remains an important historical and active military site today.

The Hard

The Hard in Portsmouth is a historic waterfront area that has long served as a vital hub for naval activity and trade. Originally a natural landing spot for ships to dock and unload, it became known in the 18th and 19th centuries for its bustling atmosphere filled with sailors, dockworkers, and "mudlarks" scavenging the shore. Today, The Hard remains a key part of Portsmouth's maritime heritage, housing attractions like the Historic Dockyard and HMS Warrior, and offering a glimpse into the city's rich naval history.

HMS Warrior

HMS Warrior, launched in 1860, was the Royal Navy's first iron-hulled, armoured warship and marked a turning point in naval technology. Built in response to France's ironclad *La Gloire*, Warrior was an imposing hybrid, powered by both steam and sail, and heavily armoured with a 4.5-inch iron hull. She measured 420 feet long and carried an advanced artillery battery, making her one of the most formidable vessels of her era, though she never saw battle.

Rapid advancements soon rendered Warrior obsolete, and by 1883, she was decommissioned and repurposed, eventually serving as a training ship and later an oil depot. In 1979, the vessel was saved from scrapping and carefully restored. Today, Warrior is a museum ship at Portsmouth Historic Dockyard, showcasing Victorian engineering and Britain's naval heritage

Portsmouth Cathedral

Portsmouth Cathedral, officially the Cathedral Church of St Thomas of Canterbury, dates back to 1180 when a chapel dedicated to St Thomas Becket was first built on the site. Blending Norman, Gothic, and neo-Classical architectural styles, the cathedral reflects centuries of expansion and restoration.

As the spiritual home for Portsmouth's maritime community, it holds a deep connection to the Royal Navy, hosting blessings and memorials for sailors and officers, especially during times of conflict. Today, this Grade I listed building serves as a vibrant centre for worship and heritage, celebrating Portsmouth's rich naval history with commemorative stained glass windows, artefacts, and plaques honouring naval service.

Fareham Creek

Fareham Creek has a rich history as a medieval trade hub, essential for shipping goods along the Hampshire coast and supporting trade with Portsmouth. During the Middle Ages, it enabled the movement of goods like wine, coal, and salt into the region, which were traded for local timber, grain, and leather. By the 18th century, Fareham Creek had developed into a notable shipbuilding area, its location ideal for transporting timber and other resources to Portsmouth and beyond, strengthening the local maritime economy.

Although Fareham Creek's commercial shipping use declined over time as silt accumulated, it remains an area of historical significance. Today, it is valued for leisure boating, maintaining its connection to Fareham's past as a vibrant trade and shipbuilding centre linked closely with Portsmouth's naval history.

The Round Tower, Portsmouth

An iconic fortification overlooking Portsmouth Harbour, the Round Tower was originally constructed in the 15th century to defend against invasion. It has undergone various modifications, including serving as a gun platform and later a defensive lookout. Today, the Round Tower is a cherished landmark, symbolising Portsmouth's naval heritage.

Spice Island

Spice Island, also called The Point, is a historic area in Old Portsmouth known for its vibrant, sometimes unruly past. This nickname originated in the 17th and 18th centuries when the area was packed with pubs, inns, and coffeehouses frequented by sailors, traders, and fishermen. Its lively atmosphere offered the "spice of life" for visitors, and it gained a reputation for lawlessness due to its location outside city jurisdiction. As a result, Spice Island became a haven for seafarers seeking entertainment and refreshment after time at sea.

This area also served as an important maritime hub where merchants unloaded various goods, potentially including exotic spices, as part of the broader shipping and trade network. During periods of conflict, press gangs would often roam the area, forcibly recruiting men for the Royal Navy. Today, Spice Island stands as a cultural landmark, reflecting Portsmouth's rich maritime heritage and lively historical character.

Esk Vale Guest House

Granada Road, part of Southsea's Victorian expansion, saw the construction of Esk Vale Guest House in 1860. Built during a time when Southsea was evolving into a prominent seaside suburb, the guest house reflects the architectural charm of the era, with its traditional Victorian style designed to attract the city's growing middle class and naval visitors.

Today, Esk Vale Guest House still stands as a piece of Southsea's rich history. This real guest house, located at 39 Granada Road, is owned and operated by the author of this book and his wife, offering guests a cozy stay amidst Portsmouth's historic and scenic coastal surroundings.

Eastney Beach

Eastney Beach, at the southeastern tip of Southsea in Portsmouth, was historically linked to the Eastney Barracks, constructed in the 1860s to house the Royal Marine Artillery. Initially a military area, it transitioned into a quiet public beach popular for its natural, pebbled shore and open views of the Solent. Today, it remains a favoured spot for those seeking a more secluded, rustic beach experience with remnants of Portsmouth's maritime and military history in the backdrop.

Southsea Castle

Southsea Castle, located on the southern coast of England in Portsmouth, is a historic fortification built by decree of King Henry VIII in 1544. Its construction was part of Henry's extensive coastal defence strategy, designed to protect England against potential military threats posed by France and the Holy Roman Empire. Southsea Castle was strategically positioned overlooking the Solent, the narrow strait between the Isle of Wight and mainland England, making it a crucial stronghold against naval attacks.

The castle is particularly notable for its role in the defence during the 1545 Battle of the Solent. Henry VIII himself is said to have watched his warship, the Mary Rose, sink from the castle's vantage point during this battle. Over the centuries, Southsea Castle underwent various modifications to modernize its defences, reflecting changes in military technology, particularly with the addition of artillery platforms during the Napoleonic Wars.

In the 19th century, Southsea Castle became part of the wider Palmerston Forts—a series of forts constructed along the south coast to protect against a potential French invasion under Napoleon III. Despite the absence of this invasion, the castle remained in military use through both World Wars. In 1960, Southsea Castle was decommissioned and subsequently opened to the public as a historic site. It is now recognized as a Grade I listed building, showcasing nearly 500 years of military history and serving as an important symbol of England's coastal defences.

Henry VIII

Henry VIII (1491–1547) was one of England's most famous monarchs, ruling from 1509 until his death. Notable for his six marriages and the founding of the Church of England, Henry's reign dramatically transformed the religious, political, and social landscape of England. Driven by his desire for a male heir, Henry broke from the Roman Catholic Church to dissolve his first marriage to Catherine of Aragon, establishing himself as the Supreme Head of the Church of England and initiating the English Reformation.

Henry was also a patron of the arts and significantly expanded the Royal Navy, earning him the title of "Father of the English Navy." This expansion included commissioning ships like the Mary Rose. Although he initially enjoyed popularity, his later years were marked by tyrannical rule, heavy taxation, and deteriorating health, including severe obesity. Henry's legacy endures as one of England's most impactful and controversial kings, shaping the monarchy and English history profoundly.

HMS Victory

HMS Victory is the British warship famous for serving as Vice-Admiral Lord Nelson's flagship at the Battle of Trafalgar in 1805. Launched in 1765, Victory was a first-rate ship of the line, equipped with 104 guns across three decks, showcasing the height of British naval engineering of the era. Her role in the Trafalgar battle was pivotal, securing a decisive victory over French and Spanish forces and solidifying British naval supremacy, though Nelson was mortally wounded on her deck.

After Trafalgar, Victory continued in various service roles before being retired and placed in dry dock at Portsmouth in 1922. Preserved as a museum ship, HMS Victory remains a treasured historical site, allowing visitors to explore her decks and experience a piece of British maritime history firsthand at Portsmouth Historic Dockyard.

Mary Rose

The Mary Rose served as a warship in the Tudor navy of England, commissioned by King Henry VIII and launched in 1511. As one of the first ships capable of firing a broadside, she was a technological marvel of her time. After decades of service, she met a tragic fate, sinking in the Solent in 1545 during a battle against the French fleet, in full view of Henry VIII, who watched from Southsea Castle.

The ship remained on the seabed for over 400 years until it was rediscovered and raised in 1982. Now preserved and displayed at the Mary Rose Museum in Portsmouth, the ship offers an unparalleled insight into Tudor naval warfare and daily life, featuring thousands of recovered artefacts that provide a unique snapshot of 16th-century England.

English Rose

The term "English Rose" traditionally refers to an idealized image of an Englishwoman, embodying qualities like beauty, innocence, and natural charm, often associated with fair skin, rosy cheeks, and a modest demeanour. The phrase gained popularity in the Victorian era when romanticized portrayals of British femininity became common in literature and art, depicting an "English Rose" as a symbol of pure, understated beauty.

Catherine Parr

Catherine Parr was King Henry VIII sixth and final wife, known for her intelligence, diplomacy, and efforts to unify Henry's children, which helped secure the Tudor succession. Unusually for women of her time, Catherine published books under her own name, making her the first English queen to do so. Her religious works, including Prayers or Meditations (1545) and The Lamentation of a Sinner (1547), reflected her commitment to Protestant reform and showcased her personal beliefs and intellect. After Henry's death, she remarried Thomas Seymour but died shortly thereafter due to childbirth complications. Catherine Parr's influence extended beyond her role as queen, establishing her legacy as a pioneering female author and significant figure in the English Reformation.

Meon River Canal

Before the construction of the Meon River Canal (also known as the Titchfield Canal) in 1611, Titchfield served as an important small seaport on the River Meon, enabling ships to access the Solent and facilitating local trade. However, the river's tides made navigation unpredictable, limiting the port's reliability. To improve this, the 3rd Earl of Southampton built the canal alongside the river, intending to manage the estuary by converting it into a controlled freshwater channel and enhancing surrounding farmland.

This construction ultimately led to unintended silting at the river mouth, cutting off Titchfield from seagoing access. Today, the canal remains a historical feature and part of the Titchfield Haven area, supporting a variety of wildlife and illustrating early English efforts in water management.

Stony Bridge

The Stony Bridge—historically known as the Anjou Bridge—holds significant historical ties to Titchfield Abbey and the medieval nobility associated with it. This bridge earned its name from its connection to Margaret of Anjou, who crossed it in 1445 during the celebration of her marriage to King Henry VI, hosted at the abbey. Originally likely constructed as a wooden bridge, the structure facilitated access to the abbey for both royal visitors and locals, bridging the River Meon and enhancing connectivity in the region.

By the 17th century, the bridge was reconstructed in stone, providing greater durability and enduring as a functional crossing point. It is officially recognized as a Grade II listed structure, symbolizing Titchfield's historic past and reflecting the craftsmanship of early bridge-building. Preserved as part of Hampshire's heritage, Stony Bridge continues to serve as a reminder of the region's rich ties to medieval England and the legacy of Titchfield Abbey.

Compass Rose

A Compass Rose is a symbol on maps, charts, and compasses used to display cardinal directions—north, south, east, and west—and often intermediate points such as northeast and southwest. Traditionally, it is illustrated as a circular design with decorative points radiating from the centre, each point indicating a specific direction. Originating in medieval navigation, the compass rose was essential for mariners, helping them orient their vessels at sea. Early compass roses often included a fleur-de-lis to indicate north and sometimes an ornate cross for east, representing the direction of Jerusalem.

Over time, the compass rose evolved from a simple directional tool into an intricate symbol, frequently featuring in historical and maritime art, with designs that reflect the beauty and importance of navigation across centuries.

Titchfield Abbey

Titchfield Abbey, founded in 1231 by the Premonstratensian order of canons, is located in Hampshire, England. Originally established as a medieval abbey, it served as a centre of religious life until the 16th-century Dissolution of the Monasteries under Henry VIII. After the abbey was dissolved in 1537, it was converted into a grand country residence, renamed Place House, and extensively modified by Thomas Wriothesley, the 1st Earl of Southampton. The abbey's structure was partially preserved, and its cloisters and refectory were transformed into living spaces. Today, Titchfield Abbey stands as a historical landmark, showcasing its transformation from a monastic site to a Tudor mansion and embodying the dramatic shifts in English religious and social history.

Chain Measurement

A chain is a unit of length historically used in land surveying, equal to 66 feet (20.1168 meters). Developed by

17th-century surveyor Edmund Gunter, the chain was divided into 100 links, each link measuring 0.66 feet (7.92 inches).

Ten chains make up a furlong, and 80 chains equal a mile, making it a convenient unit for mapping and plotting land. Although less common today, the chain measurement is still sometimes used in surveying, railway engineering, and for historical reference in property descriptions and maps.

Guy Fawkes Night

Observed annually on 5th November in the UK, Guy Fawkes Night commemorates the foiled Gunpowder Plot of 1605. This historic event involved a group of conspirators, including Guy Fawkes, who attempted to destroy the House of Lords and kill King James I. Traditionally, bonfires and fireworks mark the night, serving as a reminder of the failed plot and the punishment of those involved.

Bonfire

A traditional bonfire or large fire is typically used for celebration, often associated with Guy Fawkes Night in the UK. The fires symbolise the failed plot against the monarchy and are a familiar feature of British autumn festivities.

The Admiralty

The Admiralty, also known as the Board of Admiralty, was the British authority responsible for overseeing the Royal Navy from the 16th century until 1964. Originally led by the Lord High Admiral, it evolved into a board-run organization that directed naval strategy, shipbuilding, and operations. During the 17th and 18th centuries, the Admiralty played a central role in establishing Britain's naval supremacy by securing trade routes and expanding the empire.

The Admiralty was integral to key conflicts, including the Anglo-Dutch Wars and the Napoleonic Wars, as well as to innovations in naval tactics. In 1964, it merged into the Ministry of Defence, though its influence remains a core part of Britain's maritime heritage.

St. Peter's Church

St. Peter's Church in Titchfield, Hampshire, has roots tracing back to the Anglo-Saxon era, likely established around the 8th century. Initially a minster's church, it served as a key religious centre for the area. Over centuries, it underwent significant architectural changes, including the addition of a Norman-style west doorway in the 12th century and expansions in the chancel and chapels during medieval times.

The church's association with nearby Titchfield Abbey, founded in the 13th century, boosted its prominence, especially as local nobility, like the Wriothesley family, contributed to its adornment. One notable addition is the 16th-century monument dedicated to the Earls of Southampton. The Victorian era brought about further restoration, which preserved many historical elements. Today, St. Peter's stands as a blend of Anglo-Saxon, Norman, and Victorian architecture, reflecting Titchfield's religious and historical heritage.

Explore your creativity with my
Inspired by Colouring Book Series

Discover a world of artistic inspiration with my *Inspired by* series, a collection of adult colouring books crafted to spark relaxation, creativity, and a sense of wonder. From the intricate wildlife of Africa to other captivating themes, each book in the series invites you to unwind and bring vivid scenes to life with your own unique style. Perfect for enthusiasts and newcomers alike, this series offers something special for everyone looking to escape into colour.

Available on Amazon:

 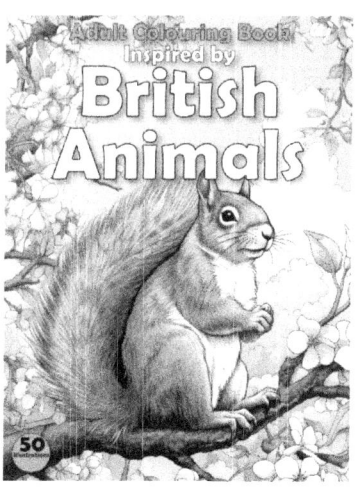

Printed in Dunstable, United Kingdom